LIFE IS HOT IN CRACKTOWN

LIFE IS HOT IN CRACKTOWN

Buddy Giovinazzo

Thunder's Mouth Press
New York

Copyright © 1993 by Buddy Giovinazzo

Published by
Thunder's Mouth Press
632 Broadway, 7th floor
New York, NY 10012

Library of Congress Cataloging-in-Publication
Data
Giovinazzo, Buddy.
    Life is hot in Cracktown / Buddy Giovinazzo.
        — 1st ed.
        p.   cm.
    ISBN 1-56025-054-2 : $19.95
    1. City and town life—New York (N.Y.)—
Fiction.   2. Narcotic addicts—New York
(N.Y.)—Fiction.   I. Title.
PS3557.I58L54   1993
813'.54—dc20   92-45666
                                              CIP

For Yvonne

CONTENTS

SPECIAL THANKS

Rose, Rick, Bob, John, and Jerry Giovinazzo,
Paul Liepa, Anne Yarowsky, Alison, Evan,
John, Jess Taylor, Phill Niblock, Antonio
Gallego, Ron & Libby, to my editor and
friend, Karen Rinaldi. And very special
thanks to Anne Stillwaggon.

LIFE IS HOT IN CRACKTOWN

Life is hot in Cracktown. The flaming sidewalk burns your feet. Steams the air, cooks the base. Blood and piss like street perfume, vaporize and melt together till your nose pukes up the residue. Cook a rat and eat him for breakfast. Fire the bazooka and he tastes like chicken. Rob the stores, the deli on the corner; take what you get, get what you take. Watch the cops sitting in their car. Shoot'em in the head when they ain't looking. Fuck the whores and make them bleed, they never cum anyway. Use the kids, good fronts, throw them candy and watch them age. The heat and pressure need to be released. On a stranger; then run. Count the money in the alley, ditch the wallet. Fire the bazooka and it feels like heaven.

Be cool. Life is cool. You're so cool. In Cracktown.

LONDA FRIES HER EGG

Pounding like a hammer on the inside of her skull, down through her spine, beating its way to her belly getting bigger by the day. Daddy's gonna notice soon, through whiskey glazed eyes he's gonna notice. He'll make her keep it. Keep it and raise it and tell her it's her own fault and she deserves everyfuckingthing that's ever happened to her cause she's a whore and a slut and a good for nothing cunt just like her goddamn fucking mother was. Then he'll beat her and throw her out cause he owes money to everyfuckingbody and he can't even show his face on the street without bumping into Caesar or Lucky-foot or Bazooka Joe on the corner selling rockets for the Colombians who would slit your throat as soon as fuck their wives.

Daddy would be up soon. Lying on the couch in his piss stained pants, too stoned to get up and go to the bathroom. She watches the cops outside from the window. Somebody must of got hurt; they're running into the alley with drawn guns. Londa stays low at the sill. She's not gonna get shot like Mrs. Cooper from standing near the window where a bullet ripped through her head and splattered the tv. The cops run back to their car and talk into the radio. She'd better start the coffee cause Daddy would be up soon and if coffee ain't ready Daddy's gonna be in an awful fucking mood. But first she opens the window and takes a deep breath, wishes her life would disappear, just dissolve into nothingness, as if everything had never existed. Or maybe if the fucking Russians would blow the whole world to kingdom come and everything'll start up all over again just like Adam and Eve except there'd be no serpents around to fuck things up and slither through the shit and slide up your cunt and put babies in your guts when you don't want them and don't want to not want them. If everything could be like that, she thought.

He better like his coffee piss weak, cause there's barely enough to make a cup. He told her to buy more last night but instead she took the five dollars and grubbed another five by sucking off Pedro's cousin Willy who she didn't have to swallow and wouldn't even if he told her to, to cop the bazooka, two blasts worth, from Pap-Smear Jones. Fuck the coffee, it's worth the beating she'll get. To fire the bazooka and say fuck the world cause I'm happy and flying like a kite and nothing else matters is the ultimate ride. Better than eating, better than sleeping, better than everything.

She turned around and he was on her like a disease.

"Where the fuck's the coffee?!" His breath shot out of his mouth like a fist of puke. "What are you lookin' at me like that for!" He popped her with the back of his hand and sent her across the room. Looking down at his knuckles, "You fuckin' cunt! You cut me!"

He had popped her open mouth with her broken chipped teeth. Her lip was bleeding, but worse, so was his hand. He ripped her from the floor and smashed her against the refrigerator; she could feel her spine quiver, the tingle in her toes. Maybe he would paralyze her and toss her out the window. From the fifth floor she'd be dead upon impact; that would do the trick, she thought. Maybe then he would be sad and realize that he really loved her and needed her and all they had were each other, the only family left; and he'd be nice and stop drinking and stop hitting her. Maybe he would realize that now before it's too late.

Instead he grabbed her head and smashed her face into the sink, slamming her forehead against the faucet where it ripped open and started bleeding down the drain. She collapsed to the floor with a bloody hand to her head as he stormed into the bathroom to change his pants. She sat for a moment holding her head with her palm, and tried to feel something, anything, but nothing ever came out: no tears or sobs or wails of pain or sorrow. Nothing. That's why he hated her so much. He said she was a heartless lying evil cunt-faced bitch just like her goddamn fucking mother was. And maybe it was true, she thought, cause she never cried. Ever.

She laughed though. Especially when the bazooka fired. When the bazooka fires everyone laughs, even people who ain't laughing laugh. The bazooka. God, she wanted it now. To load it and light it and toke it and breathe it and hold it and blow it and laugh. Laugh at Daddy, even when he's punching her; his punches feel like tickling and her blood like fuzzy velvet and the bruises decorations and his cock a magic wand.

If there was just some way to fix the coffee, to make it stronger. She was sure he would notice, he wasn't drunk yet. Not till later when he sneaks to the liquor store and buys his bottle unless he can get it on credit which he probably can't since the whole fucking neighborhood knows about him cause Caesar and Luckyfoot and Bazooka Joe on the corner selling rockets for the Colombians who would slit your throat as soon as fuck their wives have told everyfuckingbody about Daddy.

He sips the coffee, looks at her with his puffy eyes half closed like a battered boxer. She keeps her face straight and sucks in her belly, holds her breath.

"What the fuck you lookin' at, you fuckin' pig!"

Good, he doesn't notice. She goes to the sink and touches her head, the bleeding has stopped and is starting to dry. She picks at the crusty blotch on the bridge of her nose and watches it fleck in the sink.

"I want this fuckin' place cleaned up when I get back! If anybody comes for me you tell'em I'm outta town, you hear?" She nods but this pisses him off.

"What'sa matter, you got a fuckin' tongue or do you want me to rip it out for you?!"

"No. I hear you Daddy. Everything will be done, Daddy."

"It better be!"

She listens at the door as he plods down the stairs, counting each one till she hears the cracking squeal from the eleventh. Now she knows he's really on his way out and not trying to trick her so he can sneak back in and catch her not cleaning or not doing whatever he tells her so that he has every rightful reason to hit her and punch her and bang her face against the faucet in the sink. From the window, she sees him peeking out the doorway, once the coast is clear he steps out and hugs along the buildings.

Bazooka! shot through her mind. Call Pedro, let's get some bazooka. Maybe Willy's still in the neighborhood, he's good for five. Pedro can set up another one or two, then we're on line for the flight.

Before leaving, she put two tiny band-aids on her head and pressed her hair down to cover them.

"Yo Londa! It's fuckin' eleven o'clock in the morning!"

"Please Pedro. Lets get somethin', comon...."

"You a fuckin' pain in my ass, you know that, bitch!"

"I'm sorry."

"Shut up, get the fuck in here!"

He stepped away from the door and she hurried in, looking around. He was alone, no sign of Willy.

"Where's your cousin?" she asks.

"Home."

"Oh?"

"You got no shot with him."

"Huh? I sucked him good, real good."

"Your fuckin' teeth! He said it was like stickin' his dick in a meat grinder!"

"I was easy, Pedro, you know that. I never bit you or nobody!...comon Pedro, you know that!"

"Hey, what the fuck you want me to say? It's his dick, if he don't wanna stick it in your mouth, what the fuck am I gonna tell him!?...Maybe you do Parker he'll turn us on."

"Do he have?"

"He always do."

Parker was related to somebody but nobody knew who and nobody asked cause when Parker wanted you out you were gone without a clue. Just a random gunshot to the back of the head and your body would turn up in the East River floating like a bloated sack of shit face down in the water. All in all, Parker was a good sort though, always quick with a smile and a toot. Just don't fuck with him.

Londa never bit him and she never used a condom so he liked this idea of free head for turning them on. A few hits, a few jokes, some cocksucking, more hits, more jokes, more cocksucking with swallowing, more hits, some weed, two ludes each, more hits and Parker has to go.

Londa flies through the street, soaring over the gutter with her arms outstretched. Everything is perfect, life is a dream, she's so happy, fuck everything, fuck even Daddy.

She turned around and Pedro was gone. He must have sneaked away when she wasn't looking. Took the rock that Parker gave them too. Shit. Alone. On the street, even flying, she trembles. The drop is so far, and once you fall it's hard to get up. You stay down in the shit, in the cold concrete hands of shit that grab at your throat and claw at your flesh and clutch at your heart and rip it right out through your chest. She leaned against the wall and stayed there for ten minutes or four hours.

It was time for more, another shot, another hit. The taste of Parker was gone. Where's Pedro? They work together, that was the deal. He sets up the marks and she does the easy part, the part that comes naturally, the part she's been doing for seven years or half her life. Now she was on her own and if Caesar catches her, she's his.

She quickly walked to the warehouse club where they always had something going on. Passing Bazooka Joe, who asked when she's gonna cop, it occurred to her how ugly he is. With cold dark eyes on the sides of his head, he could look in two different directions if he wanted, just like a snake. Bazooka Joe, if he wasn't loaded with ammo, wouldn't get so much as a glance from the lowest-most-washed-up of whores.

Bracker lets her in and the party begins. Londa smokes their hits and sucks their dicks and kills herself inside, but that's the point. Jo Joe Cordero tries to fuck her up the ass but she squeezes tight so he pulls out and jerks off on her face. Someone kicked her in the belly but she didn't see who. Bracker lights another and everyone plays a tune as Londa does a solo on Eddie Larue—Eddie could've been white if he wasn't black.

It's late, and Daddy will be home soon, expecting his dinner even if he ain't hungry and he doesn't want to eat a thing. So Londa begs a piece for the road. Jo Joe pisses in the corner and laughs over his shoulder saying "Fuck you Londa, comere and drink my piss!" and everyone laughs except Londa cause he might be serious. They throw her a piece and she crawls on the floor and she thanks them and promises blow jobs tomorrow and leaves for the street passing Bazooka Joe who's looking more like a snake by the minute.

Daddy likes his hot dogs and if he's not too hungry there'd be one left for her. Cooking the water, she sees the flame and remembers there's something in her pocket.

"Where's the fuckin' mustard!"

She jumped to the fridge and peeked inside, how could she have forgotten the mustard? It was the little things that got her in trouble, that got her ass whipped and her teeth chipped and her pussy ripped. Daddy grabbed the mustard and wolfed down all three dogs like a toilet. He was looking at her in a weird way, something going on in his head. She held her breath and sucked her gut and made believe she was innocent.

"You havin' your fuckin' period? I mean, you look like a fuckin' bag o'shit!"

"Yeah, Daddy, it's that time of month for me. I'm sorry, I can't help it, it just happens."

"Fuckin' bleeding animals, all o'yas!"

He popped her in the belly to see if she would burst but she didn't, instead she fell against the wall and stayed there in case he wanted to pop her again. He turned and went into the other room. Holding her belly getting bigger by the day, she knew she'd have to fix it soon. Pedro can take her to the clinic or if he's tired he can get his friend Ralphie from the pharmacy on 135th to do it; she could suck him and he'd do it for free and maybe even throw in some ludes and codeine.

Daddy's staying in tonight. He's on the couch sucking his bottle. Londa has to fire the rocket but not till Daddy's fast asleep. Sit in the kitchen at the window and don't make eye contact, just gaze out at the yard. Count the rats among the garbage and pretend they're a family. Shit, a family! Tomorrow she'll tell Pedro to fix her, then she'll be able to get more bazooka cause she won't be fat and ugly and if she keeps her teeth loose maybe Willy will come back and give her another chance. She held the rocket in her sweaty palm, clutched it tightly, felt the magic in her fingertips. Soon now Daddy would be out. She wondered what mommy was doing, if she was still alive and if so what was she thinking about at this very minute. Maybe she thought about mommy when mommy thought about her and if that were true then it would be like not being alone.

Maybe if she concentrated real hard she could see mommy in her dreams, then mommy would know that Daddy's alright but still a little mean sometimes. Would mommy want her to keep it? No, probably not, cause mommy fixed two of them herself. Boy was Daddy pissed when he saw all the blood in the tub, he beat her with a belt and cut her tits with a screwdriver and tried to ram the whole thing back up there...Maybe if mommy had fired the bazooka she wouldn't have minded.

Daddy's out. Get the pipe and light it by the window and blow the smoke out in the yard for the rats. Suck in that smoke, that sweet perfume that takes your troubles and lets you pretend that somebody loves you and that you're not a piece of shit or an evil lying cunt-faced whore like your goddamn fucking mother was.

In the dark she hears the cockroaches crawl along the stove, the tap tap tapping of their feet, and in her mind they talk to her.

"Yo Londa!"

"Yeah?"

"What are you gonna tell Daddy? He's gonna say you did it on purpose, then he's gonna beat you with the belt and cut your tiny tits with a screwdriver."

"He's not gonna find out cause Pedro's fixin' it."

"Yo Londa!"

"Yeah?"

"Is it all gone? Do you have any for us?"

"You should have told me sooner, it's all gone. It's in the yard with the rats."

"You a selfish pig!"

"What's burnin'?" she hears from the couch. "What the fuck you burnin' in there?!"

Daddy stumbles in and smacks her off the chair. He turns on the light and the roaches scatter back into the stove, laughing as they go. Daddy sees the pipe on the floor and grabs it. Londa sits on the floor picking a chunk of tile from her cheek and trying to remember what room she's in.

"This is where all my money goes! You fuckin'... I struggle to survive and you be doin'...''

Daddy's face is burning, saliva drools from his mouth, he can't even speak he's so fucked up. Londa smiles and he wants to bash her jagged teeth down her throat. Instead he grabs her hair and drags her through the room where he kicks and punches her against the couch then rips her clothes off till she's completely bare. He smacks her face and bites her nipples but she doesn't cry out or make a sound, her brain tells her this can't be happening. Daddy jumps on top of her, on her rounded belly and he thrusts into her again and again till he pulls out and seeing no blood on his cock gets even angrier. He calls her names that he doesn't even know the meaning of but they come out anyway cause if they didn't he'd grab a knife from the kitchen and cut her open and throw her guts out the window. Daddy looks over at his empty bottle and thinks about smashing it over her head but changes his mind. Instead he drags her to the bathroom and shoves her face in the toilet, smashing it against the porcelain till bits of her lip get sliced off from her teeth. Doesn't matter, it's all a dream to Londa. Nothing hurts cause she's flying high and thinking of mommy who's thinking of her and as long as that's happening she's not alone. She spits out blood and spit and leans against the tub while Daddy stands over her cursing and heaving up long gooey lines of flem; Daddy's so disgusting when he's angry, it almost makes her laugh. Daddy's steel tipped shoes find their mark and make her puke but she doesn't care cause when it's over Daddy will leave her alone and she can go find Pedro and do some guys and fire the bazooka. She's bleeding from inside, it pours along the tiles and warms her legs but still she doesn't care. Someday Daddy will be sorry. Then he'll be nice and talk to her and hug her and love her and everything will be better cause there won't be any more evil lying cunt-faced Londas around to make him miserable like her goddamn fucking mother did.

Daddy told her to clean the blood and flush the toilet or else she'd be sorry. She knew she lost the baby, Daddy kicked her pretty hard. Londa began cleaning up the mess while Daddy went to the couch and lay down where he would fall asleep and piss his pants and wake up tomorrow morning to repeat the whole fucking thing all over again.

BODEGA GRAVEYARD SHIFT

Manny works hard for his wife and kids; works two jobs a day. All day long as a security guard at the Terminal Hotel where a day without blood is like a day without air. Then home to eat and see the kids. He goes to sleep and wakes at ten to man the counter at the shithole bodega with rows of dented cans of beans and rice and cheese and milk and cigarettes and beer and Lotto. He doesn't know how much longer he can work like this, it's beginning to wear on his nerves. He almost popped Concetta last week when she started in about something he didn't want to hear about. Luckily he caught himself in time. She left him alone and he really felt like shit cause he loves her and the kids, they're all that matter to him. They need him. And he'll be damned if he's gonna let them go on welfare like Fat

Tony and his mother from across the hall. So he works the graveyard shift. So far he's been lucky.

Manny went to school at first, had dreams of earning money. But then Ramon came and dreams became reality and you can't eat a cloud. When the bills piled up to Manny's neck, he didn't bitch and hit and split, he went out and got a job as a dishwasher at a fancy restaurant. On special nights he got to bring home the leftover specials; he and Concetta would play Mr. and Mrs. Trump and dine on things they couldn't even pronounce. It was rough back then but as long as he had Concetta he was happy and determined to give her something better.

A year after he was born, they noticed Ramon was different. He couldn't do certain things he should've been able to do, like sit up by himself. Funny, all the doctors had said he was fine but that's why Concetta never trusted the free clinic. Alva came next, six months after Ramon's first birthday. Manny took the security job and though it was a step up from washing dishes, he wasn't making that much more money, certainly not enough. So when Ravi from the shithole bodega mentioned he was looking for a late night worker, Manny took it. Ravi forgot to mention that he'd been robbed several times during that shift in the past few months, but knowing Manny, it probably wouldn't have made any difference. Concetta asked him how would he sleep and when would they see him if he's never home and what about the danger of being there late at night with all the crime and crack-heads, but he told her he was taking it anyway so she shut up.

Nobody comes in during the late night shift except the drunks for beer, or else a lonely pothead in need of papers which Ravi has for the obscene price of 95 cents a pack. At four A.M. Manny goes home to nap till Concetta wakes him at five and fixes his breakfast and sees him off to work.

Alva took her first step walking last month but Manny was working and didn't get to see it. Ramon may never walk, he cries all night and no matter how much food or medicine he gets he doesn't stop. Manny can see the strain this puts on his wife cause she gets as little sleep as he does. But it's worth it, he tells himself, as long as they have each other and their family. Someday they'll move out of this place cause he's been saving for a while now, yes, someday they'll be gone. The neighborhood's been changing lately; more new people—homeless beggars, drunks and junkies, strangers all—and you can't even walk the street without cracking vials under your feet and on the late night shift Manny sweeps them into the gutter so the kids can sell them back to Kenny Carter at five cents a pop.

People have been walking past the door and peering in, suspicious looking people with big eyes and dirty clothes, scratching and pinching themselves and scoping the place out till Manny looks right back at them from behind the counter and they scurry away. It can't be worth it for Ravi to stay open all night like this. There's practically no business at all. If they do twenty bucks a night it's a good night, but Manny never says anything cause if he does and Ravi agrees, then Manny's out of a job.

Concetta's sitting with Ramon in the kitchen as the sun creeps in through the shade. He's wailing and refusing to take his bottle. Manny steps in and collapses on the couch. Closes his eyes and starts to drift until his mind is pierced by the tiny shrill scream from the kitchen; if he were a different type of guy he might've killed him right then and there. Instead he goes to the kitchen to find Concetta looking half dead, her eyes are black and baggy, her mouth sagging at the ends, cheeks wet and red. It kills him to see her like this cause she's the most beautiful woman he's ever seen. He lifts Ramon from her arms and tells her to try and get some sleep and she goes inside while he paces back and forth holding his son.

"Shhhh, Ramon, comon now, don't cry," he whispers in a soothing tone. "Mamma's resting and you should be too. Shhhh, close your eyes..."

But Ramon belts out another piercing yelp and for a moment Manny thinks of chucking the whole goddamn bundle out the window: Instead he hugs him tight and kisses his face and hates himself for even thinking this for a second. It's not the baby's fault, he says to himself, he didn't ask for Down's Syndrome. Alva starts crying in her crib and before Manny can go inside, Concetta carries her into the kitchen. They look at each other with helpless tired faces and Manny feels like less of a man than usual. This is all his fault, he thinks, cause he's stubborn; his fucking pride is holding them down. He could be making great money, more than he could ever make on his own, just by working for Luckyfoot. He wouldn't have to sell it or touch it, just drive it from one place to another and let the zooka boys deal with it. But Manny won't do that, that's not the way he was brought up, so he stands in his tiny kitchen at five-thirty in the morning holding his screaming son while his wife teeters on the edge of a breakdown.

Concetta feeds Alva and lets her roam the floor then hands Manny a jar of warm strained peaches for Ramon who finally starts to eat. She takes him from Manny's arms and tells Manny to get some sleep and she'll wake him in a half hour. Manny kisses her and in his mind apologizes for the way everything is.

When he wakes the table's set, his coffee's poured and breakfast ready. Alva sits in her high chair playing with her bottle and Ramon is sleeping in his crib and all is quiet. If only it could be like this all the time, Manny thought, watching from the couch. He got up, put on his uniform and sat down to breakfast while Concetta turned over his eggs. Alva was making sounds but not yet words; soon though, he thought, she'd be talking and learning and drawing and going to school and helping her mother cook and clean and take care of her brother. She was smart, that Alva, you could tell even now, the way she studied things, her eyes absorbing everything they saw, like a sponge. Yes, she was gonna make them both very proud. Sitting at the table with his wife on one side and daughter on the other, Ramon sleeping and quiet, the jobs don't seem so hard to Manny, the hours not as long. He kissed his wife at the door, brushed the hair from her face and told her to get some sleep now that the baby was quiet.

They needed a vacation, some kind of break, anything to get away for a few days, just the two of them. Concetta's mother was coming in from Puerto Rico this spring. She could watch the kids while they go off for a few days, even if it's just to a motel in Jersey. Manny woke up two stops before his and wiped his eyes, ignoring the beggar with the styrofoam cup. He walked down Eighth and saw a young girl from the Hotel wearing a micro-mini leaning into a car where you could see halfway up her crack. Room 419, he remembered. She lives there with her mother and three younger brothers. Manny wondered if her mother knew what she was doing till he reached the Hotel and saw her watching her daughter slip into the car.

Concetta cleaned from the moment she opened her eyes. She may have been living in a tenement but it was going to look like a palace when Manny got home. Alva sat in her chair while her brother writhed and wailed in his crib. Concetta scrubbed the floors and cleaned the walls and polished the furniture and made the bed. She held her baby and gently rocked him in her arms till he fell off to sleep. Now if only Alva would sleep then she could too, but Alva was wide awake. She smiled and garbled at her mother then grabbed her bottle and shook it in her hand. Concetta lifted her out of the chair and walked her around the kitchen holding her up by the arms; Alva's feet were getting steadier, her balance more precise, soon she'll be walking on her own. Alva's such a good girl, Concetta thought, what a blessing to be around and take care of. They'd all be better off without Ramon. She stands over the crib watching him sleep and she wonders what kind of life he'll have; it's hard enough getting through being normal, but looking down at her son with his twitching eyes and spastic limbs she wants to cry. She wants to touch him and cure him and hold him close and smother him with love and kisses cause he's a beautiful boy, just like his father, and whenever she sees him she thinks of Manny, but God, he's got everything going against him in this life. She remembered when she was carrying him how her sister Marie told her to fix it, said she was too young to be a mother, that at sixteen a girl should be out having fun, not stuck with one guy. Marie liked Manny, she just didn't want to see her sister trapped like she is now. Manny never knew any of this. He was too busy dropping out of school and getting a job and taking care of Concetta and treating her like a queen. But that's what Marie could never understand.

Manny waits out front for the cops to arrive. The car pulls up with flashing lights and he leads them inside to the lobby where he tells them it's in room 712. They start for the elevator but he tells them it doesn't work and they look at each other with disgusted faces; Manny shrugs his shoulders. They proceed up the stairs. A group of kids on the first floor landing scatter at the sight of them. In 712, the wife is hysterically crying as she's holding their infant child. The guy is out on the bed with the hypo still in his arm and his bone dry eyes locked open.

"Shit, must of been arsenic," one says to his partner then asks Manny if this is how he found him and Manny says the wife came running down and that he was dead already.

"Alright, close off the room till the ambulance arrives."

"Ambulance?"

"They have to pronounce him dead, not us."

The other partner tries to lead the wife out but she fights and screams and makes a scene until the hall is full of nosy peering faces. Manny tries to keep them away but as the word spreads through the building more and more people squeeze by to catch a glimpse of the body; you'd think they'd never seen a dead body before.

Walking from the subway on his grimy street, Manny passes the shithole bodega and waves to Dusty Jones, the evening guy, then heads on over to his building. The zooka boys sit on the stoop and goof on him as he passes, they call him Mr. Security in His Monkey Suit, but he just laughs and keeps it light. He knows someday they'll all be lying in the gutter with their brains shot out, so he let's them enjoy themselves while they can. Tiny Pinto spits in his path and Manny stops and turns around with a glare and they all stare back as if to fight but after a second Manny just turns and walks away as they jeer and hoot after him. If Tiny Pinto were a little older Manny would've kicked his ass—Tiny Pinto, at twelve years old, was making more money in two days just by acting as the go between, than Manny does in two weeks.

Ramon is crying constantly, all through dinner all the time. Concetta tries to feed him but he won't eat, he only cries. Manny tries to nap but can't with all the noise; his head is splitting, his eyeballs ache and his stomach knots. He changes his clothes and tells Concetta he can't take it anymore and that he has to get out for a while. What about sleep, she asks him, how can you go to work without any sleep? He answers who the fuck can sleep with him screaming like that. She says it's not Ramon's fault and she'll hold him in the other room to keep him quiet but Manny tells her not to bother cause he's going out. Concetta gets pissed and yells it ain't fair and being home is no fucking picnic having to cook and clean and take care of the kids and if he thinks it's so easy he should try to do it himself, but he tells her to shut her mouth and get out of his face. As he starts to leave she screams out his name and he explodes in her face and the veins in his neck scare the hell out of her. She backs away as Alva starts crying in her chair while Ramon lets out a screechifying wail that rips through Manny's brain.

"SHUT THE FUCK UP YOU FUCKING..." He struggles to say something else but nothing comes out except a web of saliva dripping down his chin. Concetta steps over and pushes him away from the crib and tells him to get out and go do what he's gotta do cause one of these days he's really gonna kill Ramon and then it will be too late. Manny looks at her tear-filled eyes and her tired face and he wants to apologize but he's too fucking pissed, so he quietly leaves the apartment as Alva and Ramon wail in harmony.

He walks around the block five times, trying to unwind. Not enough time in the day, he thinks, that's the problem, there's just not enough time. He watches the cars pull over at the corner as Bazooka Joe exchanges rockets for cash. The zooka boys are out but they say nothing and it's a good thing. Finally he steps into the shithole bodega to hang out with Dusty Jones. Dusty works till midnight then he goes to cop his dust, but Ravi doesn't mind as long as he doesn't smoke while he's working. Dusty never killed anybody and swears that dust is peaceful, that it mellows him out and that's why he doesn't fuck with rockets and horse and ice and X, and as long as he has dust and is cool it's nobody's business but his own. Manny tells him he'll take over now and Dusty checks his money to make sure he has enough to cop, grabs his jacket and leaves. Great, Manny thinks, three extra hours of work, another 21 bucks. Old Man Edwards comes in and tries to buy some beer and Lotto but wants to pay with stamps and Manny tells him he can't. Pissed and cursing through withered lips Old Man Edwards gets some powdered milk and a loaf of bread. Manny tries to apologize but Edwards doesn't want to hear it. The radio scratches out a salsa tune as Manny loads the freezer with more beer. He sweeps the floor and dusts the shelves and rings up several Lotto numbers, then hangs out behind the counter waiting for the night to pass. The street is quiet tonight, no screaming and yelling or fighting or sirens wailing, and that's never a good sign. Several kids come in and browse near the freezer eyeing Manny and whispering as Manny keeps his hand on the wooden club under the counter. This time they decide to leave without taking anything. Manny thinks about calling Concetta and telling her how sorry he is and how much he loves her and Ramon and would never do anything like what she accused him of possibly doing. But he didn't want to call up Tony's mother to go get her from across the hall, and thinking this, it occurs to him how he can't even afford a phone, while Fat Tony doesn't work or do nothing but sit around eating and watching tv, yet he has a phone, a color tv, a full refrigerator and a VCR.

By midnight the streets are overflowing. The hookers are hooking and dealers are dealing and the kids make their sales to the white guys from Jersey and everything's going on as usual and life just passes him by as he sits on his perch in the shithole bodega. Nobody on the street is clean this time of night, he thinks. They're all carrying iron and shit and works and just waiting for somebody or something to look at them wrong for the action to really heat up. Through the window he watches Tiny Pinto run in and up and down and out a dozen times in twenty minutes. God, the money exchanging hands, so much fucking money; and everybody has it except him.

By two-thirty the smoke is so thick you could choke on it. Everybody's out of their fucking minds, laughing and begging for more, carousing past the window and looking in and Manny's on his guard cause tonight there's something in the air besides smoke. Pedro walks past the door pulling Londa by the arm and she looks all fucked up with her puffy eyes and bleeding lips and she can barely stand let alone walk but Pedro drags her to a group of guys and they all disappear between two buildings. The pay phone rings but it's a wrong number. Somebody comes running in hysterically, sees Manny with the phone and screams that it's for him, rips the phone from his hand and starts barking into it.

Manny watches as the guy flips out, holding his sides and doing a dance like he has to take a wicked piss. He screams into the phone that he has the fucking money and if you don't meet him where he says he's gonna find you and rip your fucking lungs out. Then he screams out a laugh and slams down the phone as Manny stays behind the counter with his hand on the club. The guy takes a good look at Manny then dashes out the door. He stands on the street wildly looking back and forth, grabs his crotch and heaves up in the gutter, then turns and comes back in the store. Manny lifts out the club but before he can raise it, he's staring into a pistol pointing at his face.

"Gimme the fuckin' money, man! GIMME IT!!!"

Manny opens the register and reaches for the cash when,

"DON'T DO IT YOU FUCK!!!"

The guy pulls the trigger but the gun clicks harmlessly. Manny jumps to the floor but the guy pulls the trigger again and this time it fires and the bullet whizzes past Manny's face missing by an inch. He crawls into the back room as the guy rips the money from the register and takes off out the store. Manny hears everyone scream and jump for cover as the guy runs down the street with his gun waving in full view. Manny's heart is pounding like a jackhammer, he can't breathe, there's not enough air, and he's clutching his chest and trying to slow himself down cause he thinks he's having a heart attack. He hears the bell over the door clang a dozen times as footsteps rush in and voices yell and as he lies there trying to live, everyone loots the shithole bodega clean. The Lotto machine spits out numbers till it jams. Manny lifts himself and stumbles into the front room but one of the zooka boys kicks him in the balls and throws him to the floor. A scream is heard from down the block followed by several shots and people running screaming calling cheering and the whole fucking world is going crazy as Manny lies there holding his balls and crying from fear and pain and hopeless hate cause he wants to kill somebody, wants to kill somebody bad.

The cops come by and Ravi's pissed as shit and yelling about how they don't protect anything and how can he run his business in this shithole neighborhood if the cops let the animals run wild. By now Manny was feeling better but went home holding his chest in case it started pounding again. Concetta was hysterical when she heard the news and hugged him and kissed him and sat him down and gave him warm milk and told him he wasn't going to work that day. She told him to quit the graveyard shift cause it ain't worth it and what good is the money if he's dead. But when he went to quit Ravi gave him a two dollar raise and at nine bucks an hour Manny was back. Ravi said enough is enough and if the fucking cops won't protect his place then he'll do it himself and so he bought a .45 semi from one of his Malaysian friends and kept it armed and under the counter in case anybody tries to fuck around. Manny didn't object.

But now when Manny walked the street the zooka boys were different, their goofs had gotten meaner, their laughter more threatening. Manny never saw who kicked him in the store but he thought it was Kenny Carter and Kenny would be the first one he gets, yes sir, Kenny's gonna wish he was born in Cleveland.

Before he left for work each night he kissed his wife and held her close and told her how much he loved her—he wasn't taking any chances. And things stayed calm for a while until last night's shift when Manny came in to relieve Dusty at quarter to 12. Dusty started talking about shit that Manny never knew before, like how Ravi was no innocent storeowner trying to earn a living by staying open all night. According to Dusty, Ravi's brother was involved in some kind of money laundering scheme where he had to have an alibi in case the cops arrested him. That's when Ravi would tell them that his brother had been working all night at his shithole bodega. Dusty probably wasn't explaining it right—and who the hell listens to anything Dusty says anyway—but the fact that Ravi pays so much for them to stay open sure made it all the more believable. Ravi was losing money by staying open.

Manny's really tired tonight, he barely got any sleep at all. Last night he did his wife, closed his eyes and Ramon and Alva sang their hearts out for an hour. Before he knew it he was at the Hotel sleepwalking through the garbage and the smell and the scum and the screaming and from the screams at home and the screams at work Manny had one giant scream building inside of him. But he kept it under control. He even stopped planning on how he would get Kenny Carter and beat his fucking brains into a mushy red pulp. It just didn't seem worth it. The fridge at the bodega was nearly empty cause there's been no order in weeks, only two cans of Old English and a six of Bud. Manny got tired of telling people they were out of things but Ravi seemed determined to let the shelves rot.

It sounds like firecrackers at first and that's what's so tricky about the whole thing. Fired bullets never sound like what they're supposed to. People are screaming and diving under cars and closing doors and every window is empty except for Manny's cause he's peeking over the sill and clutching his piece and keeping it warm and ready for somebody or something to attack. After seven shots an old woman from an upper floor sticks her head out the window and starts screaming at these kids as if they're her own. They split in all directions and take their guns with them. Manny lets out a sigh of relief cause nobody got hurt. But he thinks about the stray bullets, the ones that get fired who knows where. He grabs the phone and calls Tony's mother and tells her to get his wife from across the hall. He tells Concetta what happened but she didn't even know about it cause the tv was on and Ramon was crying. She starts in about quitting again cause she says it sounds more dangerous than ever. The cops finally drive by but nobody's hurt or bleeding in the street and there's no reason for them to stop and ask questions cause they won't get answers anyway. Manny rings up five bucks in Lotto and it strikes him as funny that an hour after a gunfight in the street everybody acts as if this were paradise.

The doctor has Ramon on something new and he's never been so calm or quiet before. He sleeps normal without the twitching and spazzing and Concetta looks like a teenager again now that she's been getting some sleep. It makes Manny want to make love to her every minute that he's home. The extra money from the shithole bodega makes a big difference too cause now they can buy more food and Manny can put away a little extra each week towards escaping. Alva hobbles around the kitchen on rubber legs while Ramon lies in his crib staring at a plastic bird hanging from the ceiling. Manny sits with his wife on the couch and sticks his tongue in her ear and she giggles and touches him all over which makes him hard. She gets up and puts Alva in her crib while they sneak off to the bedroom. Behind closed doors Concetta was an animal and she does Manny like he's never been done before cause she puts everything into it, gives herself heart and soul, and while he's seeing stars and feeling dizzy, he thinks of all the assholes on the street smoking and shooting up cause they got no one to make them feel this way, so they try to steal it through chemicals.

On his way home from work he bought her a rose from a sidewalk Moonie. She took it and smelt it then put it in a glass on the table and looked at him as if he just gave her a diamond ring. Her smile gave him energy that made him want to explode. After dinner they made love and lay together intertwined. Manny couldn't remember the last time he felt so peaceful.

When he went to work that night the freezers were full and the shelves were stacked; Ravi must've had a change of heart. Dusty was standing in an empty box cursing that Manny was ten minutes late which meant Dusty had to be straight ten minutes longer than he wanted to. Manny took his spot and waited. Tonight was slow. After an hour he sold two six packs, cigarettes, Lotto, condoms, candy and gum. The phone rang twice but nobody was there. A rat ate into a box of oatmeal and Manny had to scare it away. He drank some coffee and looked out the window and the whole block seemed peaceful. Even the whores were sitting on the stoops and not standing in the street.

At about half past two Fat Tony comes in and buys three packs of Luckys cause Tony has lungs of steel. And smelling like a bad year wine he leans his big belly on the frayed edge of the counter and starts spewing about the fucking moolinyans who work for his friends from Queens. He's spewing loud and thick and things come shooting from his mouth so Manny has to turn his face every time Tony says a P. Tony leaves and Manny takes a breath of air. Somebody's beating a hooker but it's none of his business. He thinks about his wife. A gang of kids come tearing past the store. There's yelling and screaming and lights pop on in windows and everybody looks out and Manny runs to the door to see a bunch of guys beating on a woman down the block. They drag her to the gutter and rip off her clothes and as her long blond hair is pulled off he can see that it's a man. He goes back inside and lifts the gun, feels the weight, the coldness, the power. There's something about having a gun in your hand. He puts it down as a car pulls up; somebody gets out and comes in. A big brawny guy in an army coat with a friendly face Manny's never seen before. He steps over to the fridge and makes like he's looking for something but he's really checking the place out. He turns to Manny and asks if there's any cottage cheese and when Manny tells him no he looks disappointed and heads for the door. Before reaching it he grabs into his coat and rips out a gun and points it at Manny's face. Manny freezes and the guy seems real calm about it, not like the last guy. He softly tells him to open the register and as Manny does the guy sneaks a glance at his car out front, still running. Then he gently reaches into the register and empties it, takes the tray and drops it to the floor but there was nothing underneath. He asks where the rest is and when Manny tells him that's all there is, he doesn't look too pleased. Manny didn't move his hands from above his head and the guy was looking right at him. Manny wasn't gonna wait to get his face blown off so he tells the guy there might be more in the back room, then throws a glance towards the front door. When the guy looks over Manny grabs the gun under the counter and in a flash squeezes the trigger and feels the jolt and through the wisp of gray smoke the guy has half his neck blown away. You could see the bone and tubes inside. The guy clutches his throat and gurgles something out before falling to the floor. He tries to crawl out the door but collapses two feet later and just lies there oozing like a toilet overflowing. Too stunned to move from behind the counter, Manny looks up at the ceiling, at the thick cloud of smoke hovering near the lights. People run past and call to their friends, peeking in the window with wide excited eyes but nobody comes in once they see Manny standing there with the gun in his hand. He slowly steps around and sees the guy's hand still clutching the gun. He lifts it from the floor and immediately knows something's wrong. The gun comes up and floats to his face like a feather, it's empty, hollow. Fucking plastic! And Manny stares at it in horror. There's a scratch in the side and a bright orange color shows through the black paint. Holding it in his hand he can't believe how fake it looks and shit, why didn't he notice this sooner. By now there's a crowd outside and they're all staring and talking and laughing like it's a block party and Manny just stands there as the pool of blood grows around his feet. He thinks he sees the guy's fingers move. There's no way out of this for Manny. Self defense or not, unlicensed gun versus plastic, he's gonna be sent up cause Bernie Goetz ain't too popular in Cracktown. And seeing Kenny Carter's grinning face through the window laughing with his zooka boys, Manny thinks of making a clean sweep of it, of taking them all out by blowing the smiles off their fucking faces and show-

ing them he's not gonna take it anymore and who
are they to run the world and destroy everything
and make up the rules on how life should be lived.
But then the siren turns the corner and the zooka
boys take off and as their car stops in front and the
cops get out, Manny thinks of calling Concetta, but
by now it's too late.

MISS LONELY HAS A DATE TONIGHT

Miss Lonely has a date tonight, a one shot deal for the evening. Caesar set it up cause he said she's his special girl. No roundabout cockathon tonight. No sir. One man, one cock. Yes, this was a special night. And if Miss Lonely does good and her mark tells Caesar how fantastic she is and how much he wants to see her again, she'll be off the street and in the club. That's success. No more fighting over corners and vying for dollars, strictly high class work from now on. But she'll have to do whatever this guy wants tonight, whatever he says. She's gonna touch him and lick him and suck him in places he didn't know he had, he's gonna be having some serious visions of heaven and earth and fire and hell and maybe he's connected and will turn her on all night as long as she does him right.

She fixed her makeup and touched up her eye, dabbing powder over the bruise where Lucille popped her for sucking off her husband Hector. He paid, what could she do? But Lucille didn't want to hear it. Anyway Caesar worked it out and made Lucille apologize and they shook hands. Then Lucille took the park while Miss Lonely took the bridge, which was Caesar's way of thanking her for not making a big thing out of it.

She better hurry, Caesar wants to see her in twenty minutes. She fixes her garter and slips on her panties and dabs some cheap perfume but not too much cause tonight she has class. Caesar's gonna be so proud, he's gonna know he made the right choice. She's gonna do him right.

"Get in Bitch!"

His hair flashed like diamonds and his teeth were chunks of gold. He had so much class in his gray silk suit. Next to him Miss Lonely felt cheap but she hoped he wouldn't notice.

"You do this guy special tonight, you hear? It's important."

"I'll make it special for him, I'll be real nice."

"He's very important to me, you hear? You do whatever he wants. You swallow his cum, you lick his ass, you fuck him sideways, whatever the fuck he wants you do. If he don't want no scumbag you don't use one, you hear?"

"Yeah Caesar, I know what to do. I'm gonna do you right Caesar, then you see I can work inside too. I know how they like it, I know how to..."

"Shut the fuck up!"

Miss Lonely watched him as they drove downtown. If only he would fuck her, she thought, cause he never ever fucked her. He might even want to keep her all for himself. Then she'd be in like gold. All the girls would be jealous and say things like what the fuck could she do different than us? What makes her pussy so special? She's just a cheap nigger bitch like the rest of us...shit, that's what they would say. If only he would fuck her.

Caesar fired the bazooka but didn't toke, he passed it around and she gulped it and held it till her lungs collapsed, then blew it out the window. Caesar lit another and she was feeling fuzzy. They were cruising all the high class hotels and she couldn't believe she'd be working down here tonight. If only Lucille could see her now, boy would she be pissed. Lucille's working the park tonight where she does the winos and junkies with all kinds of diseases and scabs on their dicks, coughing and puking. It's enough to make you want to quit and move away. But you would never do that, how else could you get the bazooka?

The car pulled over to a big green place and a square man in a red wooden uniform stepped over.

Miss Lonely tingled inside, her stomach jumped, her head was spinning and she was wet and hot and ready to fuck a subway car. Caesar gripped her chin and with his thumb wiped a speck of lipstick smeared from the pipe, then checked her teeth.

"Listen Baby, I'm counting on you tonight, you're my special girl tonight. If you do this right, I'm moving you inside, you hear? You gonna have money and zooka, I'll be turning you on to anything you want and nobody's gonna fuck with you cause if they do they'll have to fuck with me. Alright Baby, this is your chance, don't let me down."

"Thanks Caesar, I won't be lettin' you down, you'll see how good I do...you'll see..."

The door opens and Miss Lonely goes to climb over when Caesar stops her.

"Where you going? This place ain't for you."

The driver, Jimbo, looks in the rear view mirror with a smile. Caesar looks at him and laughs.

"You believe this shit, Jimbo, she thinks this is for her!"

They're both laughing now. Miss Lonely watches them.

"Yo, this is for me, bitch! Jimbo's taking you to your place. You think you can even walk into a place like this? They'd throw your fucking ass out before you hit the door."

Caesar gets out of the car, then turns back inside.

"Remember, you do whatever he wants. You hear?"

Miss Lonely nods her head.

"Caesar...could you give me somethin' to get me back up? I need somethin' to lift me back up, just a small piece. I was feelin' so fine a minute ago but just a small piece to get me back up..."

"Fucking Bitch, you fuck this up and I swear I'll hurt you bad, I'll hurt you so bad you won't be working no more."

Caesar tosses a small rock on the seat and she grabs for it between the cushions. Jimbo pulls away.

A minute later she's back in the clouds and feeling like a queen. Jimbo sneaks a glance at her in the mirror but she ignores him. She'd never fuck Jimbo, he's just a driver, so if he's got any ideas he might as well forget them cause the only way he's getting any is if Caesar tells her to. She was amazed that all the stores would be open this late. Where she lives nothing's open this time of night but down here everything's open, stores and boutiques and shops and restaurants and theaters and the streets are packed with people walking and talking and doing things. Nobody down here could get any bazooka though, cause she didn't see anybody hanging out with any to sell, unless they were in disguise or else they only sell to their friends. The farther down they drove the straighter she became until she wished that Caesar gave her a bigger piece so she could get back up. Jimbo kept looking at her with a stupid grin. Maybe he was carrying, she thought. That's why he keeps looking; maybe he's waiting for her to ask so he can make a deal.

"Jimbo, you got somethin'?"

"Sure I got something. What's it to you?"

"Jimbo, you turn me on and I'll do you, we pull over under the bridge right here and I'll do you good."

"I don't need no whores, I got plenty o'bitches!"

"Just a taste, Jimbo, please, I'll do better for Caesar if I'm up. If I'm up I'll do him right. Please..."

"Fuck you and shut up!"

Jimbo drove over the bridge and she asked him where they were going but he wouldn't answer. She sat back and slugged a bottle of whiskey from the bar till Jimbo saw her through the mirror.

"You get fucking sick and I'll beat your fucking face in, Bitch!"

"It's just a sip, Jimbo, just a sip to get me up. I know how to do what Caesar wants. I'm one of his best."

"You're one of his worst! You're a fucking washed up sleazy cunt and if it wasn't for his charity you'd be sucking rat dicks at the dump."

"That's a downright fuckin' mean thing to say

to me, Jimbo. If I ain't special why would Caesar gimme this special job that's so important to him?"

"You'll find out. Now shut the fuck up before I throw you over the side."

Miss Lonely watched him in the mirror but turned her eyes when he looked back. "You won't be throwin' me over no side," she muttered under her breath. "Not with Caesar wantin' me to do this job."

"Shut the fuck up!"

They drove over the bridge in silence until they hit a highway in an outer borough.

"Where we goin', Jimbo. I never been down this far before. Comon, tell me, please."

Jimbo looked at her in the mirror and for the first time she looked concerned. Jimbo'd better relieve that.

"You're going to a special place, Bitch. This guy has his own place, you gonna like it."

Then he reached into his dirty shirt pocket and tossed back a rock.

"Oh thank you Jimbo, I owe you one good. I'll do you good, you see. I'm gonna tell Caesar how good you are to me."

"Yeah, you do that!"

The roads got darker, Miss Lonely got higher, and Jimbo got quieter. Yeah, this was a special night. She was prepared for anything. She'd done it all before, been fucked and sucked and touched and felt and hit and whipped and pissed on and pissed on others. Once she shit on a white guy from Brooklyn—that was real disgusting, the only time in her life that she gagged. Caesar made him pay triple and gave her an extra piece. But this guy tonight must have class, he won't want to be shitted on, not if he's having her brought to his own place. Maybe he's important, that's why it has to be so secret. Maybe he's from the government or somebody who's big like that. Sometimes when conventions are in town Caesar sets them up with all kinds of old-time white guys who only do it normal but can't be seen on the street or in sleazy hotels. Most of them only want blow jobs which are great cause you don't have to get messed or dirty, you just suck them and you're finished. Yeah, maybe that's what this would be: one quick suck for mankind, and a giant leap for Miss Lonely. This made her giggle and Jimbo looked in the mirror with a scowl. She laughed out loud and this time he smiled, looking right at her eyes as she was looking back.

Jimbo was running early, wasn't expected till 12, so he pulled over near the woods and parked the car.

Miss Lonely was still flying as she took him raw and with his hand on the back of her head she felt strapped in with no place to go, where you can't speak or scream or cry out in any way. *Alone.* She felt so alone when she worked, so empty, without a heart or a soul, like a tool that gets old and worn out but still gets used cause it's not completely worthless yet. She tried to think of other things but her mind always took her back. *Alone.* It's such a pretty word, she thought, such a fucking pretty word. *Alone,* the sound of it doesn't match the feeling of it. If she could change any word in the world, she knew it would be *alone.* She'd change it to Shit or Cock or Cunt or Fuck, something that sounds hard and cold. Jimbo moaned and clutched her neck tighter. She relaxed and closed her eyes and went far away, all the way back to her birth, where her first moments of life were spent twitching and bleeding and heaving up pure saliva as her entire body screamed for one more shot of smack. That was the first and last gift her mother ever gave her cause she dropped her load then split the scene, never to be heard from again. Miss Lonely was sent from place to place till she wound up in a government home where Julio the Janitor raped her twice a week until she was 13. She fucked her way to kingdom cum then ran away and met her first husband Oscar. Oscar didn't take any shit and if she said one word out of line she got popped in the mouth. She got popped pretty often. Oscar worked for Taco Nick—so known for having his wife spread her legs to show off her pussy while Nick would say, "Don't it look like a taco?" Oscar was running ludes and mesc and wanted to work up to blow and horse and Taco Nick said he would if he proved himself to be cool. It was Taco Nick who told Oscar to start Miss Lonely working. He told him, ''Her pussy's worth something, you should capitalize on your investments.'' It was strictly a part-time thing Oscar assured her, just till they could get a little something put away. By the fourth abortion Oscar was fed up, he kept screaming that he married a fucking baby factory. Miss Lonely fought to keep the last one, but Oscar wouldn't hear of it. Why should he be held down by something he doesn't want or have the time or the energy for, something he's not even sure is his which it probably ain't cause she's a whore and a slut who fucks twenty men a night. Miss Lonely tried to convince him that it was his, which they all were, cause Miss Lonely never fucked any man without a scumbag. The only man who did these days was Oscar. But Oscar said that was bullshit cause maybe one of the johns put a pinhole in it for a good laugh to see what comes out nine months later. When Miss Lonely told him that sounded crazy he punched her in the nose and she bled through the night. When Oscar told her to abort it the next morning she did. Maybe next time, she thought, if she can just hide it till it's too late, then Oscar might want it, or at least let her keep it.

A month and a half after the abortion that ruined her inside Oscar was shot dead in the street. He was walking to the Gator Room with Poncho Jeremiah when two kids ran up behind them and popped them both in the heads with .22s. Oscar was dead before he hit the pavement but Poncho lived for two days. Even on his dying breath he wouldn't say who he thought was involved. Miss Lonely cried over Oscar even though she hated him. She didn't want to be alone. Now there was nothing to do but split the scene cause she wasn't going to work for Taco Nick without Oscar. She went to Detroit to a sewer of a neighborhood where she got hooked back on shit. With hungry veins to feed, she went to work on the lonely auto workers.

"Easy on the teeth, Bitch! Lighten up, it's a fucking cock not a piece of wood!" She grunted and slurped as Jimbo fingered her ass.

She never married Kamel though they lived as husband and wife. He didn't care what kind of whore she was, didn't bother him at all. He worked as a cab driver but was involved in some kind of Lebanese crime syndicate. Miss Lonely never knew exactly what it was but he always had a lot of money on him and was always bringing suspicious Arabs to the apartment. She didn't care cause Kamel was good to her. He never hit her, gave her free shit, let her do whatever she wanted, and she didn't have to fuck anyone but him. It was heaven. Until Kamel wanted kids. He said he needed to have a family here, that it would look good for the green card guys. Miss Lonely tried and tried till Kamel got pissed. First he blamed it on the shit, so she quit. Then he blamed it on the dust; finally he said her pussy was poisoned and if she couldn't produce he was splitting. She begged him to stay, fucked him everyway a man could be fucked, but Kamel walked out one day and never came back. Ain't that some kind of shit, Miss Lonely thought.

Shortly after Kamel left, she met Max who set her up and gave her shit and told her if she ever stiffed or ripped him off he would cut out her pussy and nail it to her face. Now she was part of the group and could fuck and suck and shoot her veins and do whatever she wanted as long as she made her marks and gave it all to Max. Max put her up in a place with Sheila, Lorraine and Connie so they would all be close and he could keep his eye on them. Sometimes he would make Connie and Miss Lonely go down on each other while Lorraine jerked him off. Connie, at fifteen, had been working for Max for three years and though a street whore, she had smooth soft skin and perfect white teeth and a body that rivaled the most buxom of babes. Miss Lonely thought Connie was the most beautiful thing she'd ever seen and when Connie hugged her and kissed her and touched and licked her all over for Max, Miss Lonely thought she would die from happiness. They fell in love and worked together, held hands and watched out for each other. When Max would hit one the other would step in and get hit too but it was okay as long as they were getting hit together. Then Max would hit Sheila and Lorraine and tell them they should be like Connie and Miss Lonely and stick together cause there's a lot of sick motherfuckers out there just waiting to get their hands on sexy bitches.

One night Connie and Miss Lonely were out at the yard on a slow night. The factories and warehouses were closed for some holiday and they had only done half of what they normally do and they knew Max would be pissed cause he didn't want to know about holidays, he just wanted the money. They started to flag down cars from the road and Connie was flashing her tits. Miss Lonely had tiny little things compared to Connie's and nobody would stop for her sagging peaches, so she stood off to the side lifting her skirt and flashing some pink. A big green car pulled up and as Connie and Miss Lonely stepped over, the driver called out, "Just the one with the tits!"

Miss Lonely stopped and held Connie's arm. "I don't like this one, Connie, let him go."

"No, we can't. We gotta have something tonight, I'll just suck his dick and be out."

Miss Lonely stood off with burning eyes as Connie got into the passenger side. The car pulled away and parked along the railing. Miss Lonely watched the whole time, but there was something wrong about this one: the look in his eyes, it was no sex look, it was a cold, dangerous look, and the knot in her stomach made her aware of how foolish it all was. It's not worth it, she thought. Now that she has Connie and they love each other and they live together as wife and wife and no one is the boss and no one hits the other and they do everything together and shoot for each other, why are they even bothering with all these fucked up guys who only want to hurt them with their cocks? They could move away and get jobs together and work like normal people and buy their shit instead of getting it from people like Max. Nobody would ever have to know what they used to do and even if people did know who gives a shit cause they're together in love and not alone. Suddenly the car screeched away and disappeared down the road. Miss Lonely ran after the car screaming out Connie's name and cursing the driver, trying to see what direction they were going but she couldn't cause his lights were out and it was too dark. She tried to flag down a car but none would stop except for two guys who tried to run her over. Everything inside her started rushing out. Her whole life swept in front of her and her stomach puked up the loss. She was lying in the street crying like an animal, calling for Max but not out loud;

calling as if he were some kind of mystical spirit who would hear her no matter where he was. One car stopped and the driver got out but once he saw her tiny skirt and garter, he got back in and drove away. Shortly after, Max drove up in his black Saab, pissed as shit, not knowing what the fuck happened only that something did. Once Miss Lonely spit it out through tear stained lips he took her head and banged it against the hood. They jumped into the car and took off to rescue Connie except this wasn't like the movies. Miss Lonely knew that Connie was now concerned with higher things, beyond this world; cause you don't return when somebody takes you away like that, especially if you're nothing but a worthless piece-of-shit whore. After a few days when Connie never turned up Max said enough already it's time to get back to work and quit your crying. He tried to convince her that Connie ran away and that the whole thing was a set-up so that he would think she was kidnapped and wouldn't go out looking for her. Max gave Miss Lonely every kind of drug he had until she was too fucked up not to believe him. Sheila held her up on the street and helped her into the cars cause once inside she could do what she had to do lying down. She tried to snuff herself twice, once by shooting bad shit, the other a sloppy attempt to slice her wrists. The second time Max beat the fucking shit out of her for messing up the bed with puddles of blood. He told her that if she's gonna die it's gonna be slow and painful and not by her hand but by his. Then he told her he tracked Connie down and knew where she was and that she was living with a man and didn't want anything to do with her cause she was a fucked-up lesbian bitch. He pulled something out of his pocket and told her to try it; he said it was better than basing. She did. And it was. She'd found her God— that sweet minty smoke that sweeps through your lungs and shoots through your heart and fills up every crevice and hole in your body. It seeps into every cell and fiber and fills you with warmth and awareness and you're racing yet dragging and flying but running and everything's happening at once and that's the reason you keep doing it. Bazooka. You're not alone when you're flying high and every man becomes a little more bearable.

Fuck Connie, she would say when she was blitzed out of her face, who needs that little bitch if she wants nothing to do with me.

Fuck Connie, she would cry when she came down, we loved each other, we were perfect together. God I want her and need her and God I can't take being alone in this fucking place. *Alone.*

Jimbo was thrusting into her harder and harder and she was trying to keep from choking. As she got straighter she could feel the holes opening up inside, the hollow veins shriveling up because there's no one and nothing to fill them with. *Alone.*

"Comon you fuck, put some suction on that thing!"

She cried, softly at first, but then sobbing, her tears falling on his pants.

"Now what the fuck! What are you, out of your fucking mind?! You're sucking a fucking cock and you're gonna start crying?!"

She tried to speak but he held her head tight.

"Just make me cum and I'll drop you the fuck off! Fucking lunatic whore!"

She tried but Jimbo wasn't cumming. She sucked him for twenty minutes without a breath but still he wasn't any closer.

"Comon, lighten up! What the fuck you doing?"

If only Caesar could see her now, she thought, see her with Jimbo here in the back seat when they're supposed to be working. Caesar wouldn't take this lightly. He'd beat the shit out them both except she wouldn't mind cause she's used to it. Jimbo would be ashamed and every time she'd look at him he would remember the time he got his ass kicked good because of her. Caesar was rough but he certainly didn't hit her as much as Max did, but Max was much freer with the shit. When she worked for Max she was always burning rockets or shooting veins or doing whatever she wanted cause that was

Max's way of keeping her. But leaving Max was not easy either. He nearly sliced her face like a pizza the first time she tried. He held a razor to her cheek and she could feel the cold steel of the blade pressing into her flesh till she cried and begged him to let her stay. Then she went out and worked two days straight without a break to prove how much she loved him and would be his best whore. Max put Sheila on to make sure she didn't split, but Sheila never liked her because of Connie. One night Sheila got some guys to rape her and rob her and beat her up so that when Max asked for her money Miss Lonely wouldn't have any. As punishment he made her do a violent party at ten bucks a fuck where three men would have her at once and she would be unconscious by the end of the night, bleeding like a pig so that Max had to take her to the hospital where they stitched up her pussy. She couldn't walk for three days. The cops came in and questioned her but she wouldn't talk. A young nurse gave her the number of a shelter but she was afraid to call. She just lay there and cried and moaned and begged for Connie and something to ease the pangs but no matter how much morphine they gave her it wasn't enough. She wanted the bazooka. Finally they discharged her and gave her a number of a clinic. Miss Lonely went out the door and was expecting Max to be waiting there so he could take her back to work but he wasn't. She stood for an hour until the pangs got too strong, then walked away. She blew two guys behind the Amtrak station, copped a rocket then hopped a train to New York where she met Caesar who told her she couldn't work alone cause nobody lets you freelance in this town. She hooked up with him and has stayed that way for the past four years.

The phone rang in the front seat and Jimbo grabbed her hair and pulled her away.

"Shit," he mumbled, "we should've been there already. You make one sound and I'll cut your eyes out!"

Jimbo leaned over the front seat and took the phone. Miss Lonely stifled her whimpers.

"No, I just dropped her off, everything's fine. Yeah, I know. I'll pick her up when you call...I'll be cruising. The radio was on, I didn't hear it till the second ring...No problem, I know what to do." Then he hung up.

"Was that Caesar, what did he say?"

"He said to shut the fuck up." Jimbo got back into the driver's seat cursing her for being a frigid cunt who can't even make a guy cum with her mouth. He pulled away as Miss Lonely wiped her face; she was no longer crying, though she hurt as much as before. Just a few more years of this shit, she thought. She's gonna work her way inside the club where she can make good money and sock it away. Then she'll get the fuck away from all these fuckheads and she'll never look at another man's cock as long as she lives. Then she'll come back when none of this matters to her and these people are strangers to her and she'll hire somebody to kick the living shit out of Jimbo till he chokes on his own bile. Two more years, tops.

Jimbo raced down the highway to drop her off before the mark called Caesar and asked where his date was. Shit, if this cheap scuzzy whore puts him in bad with Caesar he'll take her out and strangle her with his bare hands and stuff her fucking body down the sewer. He saw her in the mirror, she was a wreck. Her makeup smeared, lashes off, hair like an old broom.

"Shit, fix yourself up, you look like the back end of a bus."

She dabbed her lips and combed her hair but she still looked bad. Jimbo threw her another rock figuring if she felt better she might look better cause if the mark refuses to take her cause she looks like shit then Caesar will send Jimbo out on the street to suck dicks in her place. She took the chunk and lit it, taking long deep tokes. The change amazed Jimbo. How could she look like a rancid chunk of meat one minute and a sexy whoring bitch the next? She must've been a fine looking piece when she was younger; if only he knew her then, boy would he have fucked her good. He pulled off the road and drove down a long narrow driveway lined thick with trees. Miss Lonely had never been in the country before. Jimbo stopped about twenty feet from a small wooden cottage where a tall man in a white shirt and jeans stepped out holding a glass.

"You were supposed to be here thirty minutes ago," he said with a slight British accent. "I was about to call your boss."

"We hit some traffic," Jimbo spit out, trying to hide his terror at the thought. Miss Lonely smiled inside and for a moment thought about telling where they'd really been. Maybe then the stranger would send her away and Jimbo would have to explain it all to Caesar and wouldn't that be justice. But if she did that, she wouldn't get her chance to show Caesar how valuable she is, so she kept her mouth shut. She sat in the back seat while Jimbo and the man talked in the doorway. She couldn't hear what they were saying and didn't care either way. She was tingling, like a singer before the show, her head spinning with visions and dreams of the future.

Of Connie.

Shit, Connie. Why did she have to run away like that? Why did she say that she loved her? All their dreams and plans, everything, it was all shit. If love counts for nothing then everything else is shit. And sitting in this luxury limo with a bar and a radio and a tv and telephone and all the nice things that blood and fuck money can buy, she was still all alone. And maybe life is meant to be lived alone, maybe she was meant to be alone. No matter how much money she'd have she'd still be alone. The more she thought about it, the emptier she felt. She grabbed the scotch and slugged five gulps till her stomach caught fire. Jimbo came over and opened the door.

"Alright, you know what to do. You fuck this up and you're good as snuffed."

"Jimbo, wait a second," she said with a slur, her eyes glazed. "Jimbo, just tell me one thing. Why do you hate me?"

"What?" he said, pissed and puzzled.

"Why do people hate me? What did I do to them? Why is everybody so alone and fucked up. Why don't anybody love each other and take care of each other without runnin' away and hittin' and trashin' and lyin'."

"Don't pull this shit," he answered, glancing over his shoulder at the mark watching in the doorway, still holding his glass. "Caesar will fucking cut your heart out if you don't stop this shit right now. Now get the fuck out of the car."

Jimbo didn't want to pull her out forcibly, not with the mark there, but she refused to go.

"No, Jimbo, I want to know what it means. Why can't people find each other and live together and be a family without all the other bullshit..."

"You're drunk and fucked up, now get the fuck out of the car! Don't make me pop your face, I swear bitch, don't make me..."

"Then just tell me why?"

"Tell you what?!"

"Why does everybody have to be so alone? It's not right, it's not how it's supposed to be, is it? If everyone's meant to be alone why are there so many people in the world, and why is bein' alone so fucked up? What ever happened to fuckin' God?"

Jimbo noticed the mark waiting impatiently, he grabbed her hand but she pulled it away.

"Get out, you fucking bitch!" Her eyes started watering and Jimbo was about to shit his pants. "No, don't cry, I swear I'll fucking kill you right here and now!"

She wiped her eyes but still wouldn't budge.

"Alright, you wanna know what happened to God?" he said in hushed panic, "he's dead. He's fucking dead and buried and he never existed and everybody's alone cause that's how it's supposed to be. You're alone cause nobody can stand to be with anybody for any kind of time because everything and everybody sucks my big fucking dick and if you don't get the fuck out of the car and do this guy like you're supposed to I'll fucking cut out your pussy and mount it on the hood."

A tiny smile crossed her lips, and he thought she was completely out of her mind. He also knew it wouldn't matter in a few minutes. She took his hand and he led her out of the car and over to the doorway. She leaned against him for support, and feeling his warm body and fake concern, she realized how right he was. She looked up at the mark sipping his drink and recognized something in his eyes. The look. Not that she'd ever seen his face before but she knew those eyes. It's a universal look, and no matter how big the mouth smiles, the eyes reveal the truth. Jimbo brought her inside and sat her down on the couch. A fire burned in the fireplace and it was all some kind of abstract dream to her. Jimbo turned to the stranger, mentioned something about calling Caesar when he's finished, and left them alone. Miss Lonely watched Jimbo leave and as he went through the door, he looked back. She knew his look too, had seen that one before; though she couldn't remember where or when. The door was closed and the mark came toward her like a jungle cat, slowly, coldly, a gleam in his icicle eyes. He put his drink down and reached for something in his back pocket. The handcuffs caught the firelight...

Jimbo drove around for three hours, slugging scotch and firing rockets till he was completely blitzed. The phone rang and he lifted it to his ear before the first ring finished...

"Yeah, okay. I know what to do."

He turned around and drove back down the dark and lonely highway.

Lovers hold hands and kiss by the railing, gazing out at the water. The sun sets over New Jersey, a blood red sun that screams to stay but soon whispers into nightfall. The lovers walk along the rail and dream of their lives together and the children they would have and how much they love each other and how lucky they are to be in a world where God exists to make it possible to love each other and live your life without being alone. They reach the end of the walkway and turn around to head back when she notices something in the water. It's just a rug he tells her, just a rug somebody dumped. They walk back hand in hand and kiss against the streetlights.

NANCY NORMAL NEEDS ANOTHER

Nancy Normal needs another precious puff of smoke. She gets her husband out the door with kisses, lunch and an umbrella in case it rains. He burps his bagel, picks his nose and pats her on the ass, but Nancy doesn't care as long as he leaves. The room deflates as the door is closed. Nancy turns around and glides to the cabinet and slugs some brandy to get her through the next ten minutes. She dresses light with her stomach tight cause now it's time to hit the road. She takes a Val with scotch to get her through the tunnel, grabs her purse and pops a mint and drives to the cash machine to make another withdrawal. Her husband hasn't noticed yet cause so far she's been discreet. It's all in moderation, she thinks. But lately she's been using more. She pulls onto the turnpike as a trooper pulls someone off then she gets on the tunnel exit.

She stops at the light and the homeless charge with squeegee sticks of sponge and water and no amount of waving can get them away. When they're done it's more dirty than before but Nancy gives them a buck.

The sun is shining and it's safe in daylight. The zooka boys pay her no mind cause she's one of the regulars now, even if she looks too normal. She turns the corner and the street is bare. No sign of anyone and she starts looking for cops, thinking of reasons why she would be here in case they pull her over. She drives down the block, the whores on the stoop make her feel a little safer. The phone rings and Nancy thinks BJ is watching from one of the buildings and calling to tell her he'll be right down but then she remembers he doesn't have this number. It's her husband calling to ask where she is so early in the day and she tells him she's going to the mall to pick up some things for Thanksgiving and maybe do some early Christmas shopping. A knot grips her stomach when he tells her to use the Christmas money cause that's been gone for five months now. And shit, thinking about having a house full of his family and his fat sister Shirley from Bayonne with an accent to match, she wishes she took out another hundred cause this calls for some serious copping. She drives around the block a couple of times, passing the kids and the whores who all look over and smile cause they know why she's there. She pulls to the side and keeps her car running, waiting for something to happen. Up the block, a long-haired dread-head creature in dirty tattered clothes steps out from a building and gets into a gray Rolls Royce parked at the curb. Nancy shakes her head as it pulls away. There's a scream from behind and she whirls around with fear in her eyes and sees the kids playing with a rat in the gutter.

"Szzzup, Nance!"

He startles her at first and when she looks up he has one eye on her and the other on the kids with the rat. And though she hates when he leans in her window like this, it's the only way he conducts his trade with her. She tells him what to pass—which is four rocks more than normal—and BJ's only too happy to please cause Nancy pays ten while everybody else pays five. BJ considers it an out of state tax. He makes the switch then says she could have it all for free if she wants to perform something of a personal nature right back here in the building. Nancy tells him she'd rather fuck Frankenstein, but says it with a smile. BJ reaches into the window and cops a feel and Nancy doesn't stop him cause she wants to stay on good terms. He pinches her nipples till they get hard and Nancy looks around to make sure nobody's watching and as long as nobody is he can keep feeling. She pulls his hand away and tells him that's enough and as she notices his cock pushing through his pants towards her face, she puts the car in gear. BJ tells her not to leave him hanging like this. He offers another rock, but Nancy drives off and waves goodbye. She heads down past the lights and the sponges minus another buck till she hits the tunnel. Once inside, she checks her buy; BJ never ripped her off but you can never be too sure.

She pulls into the round driveway and goes into her square house. Once inside she goes to her special secret place in the basement, a place nobody knows about cause to anyone else it's just a corner of the basement. But to Nancy it's her church. She fires it up and drills her brain where it nestles her spine and kisses her heart and wraps around her soul. It makes her feel like she did when she was dancing, when she was good, a major talent some would say. She whirls around the room and the poles become her partners as she flies like a bird, like a phoenix in flight, like an eagle on fire, a dog in a fight. She floats up the moving wooden stairs and toes into the kitchen to start her work. Standing in this high-tech horror with its blenders and motors and toys for the bored, she realizes there's nothing for her to do. This is her life. She laughs like a girl as she skips through the house and dances with the wall unit. They do a waltz. She's down for another cause that one was spent and there's still nothing to do but dream of what went wrong.

Her husband's making money selling bonds and running deals, but he's a stranger to her now. She remembers that year in the Philippines when they both joined the Peace Corps. They had nothing but each other and they were never happier. She wonders what happened. They've supposedly been trying to have kids for a while now and lately he's been wondering if he's sterile. But everytime he wants to go to a doctor Nancy stops him and says they'll try again. Nancy won't tell him she's back on the pill cause as long as she's smoking shit she won't be having kids. Not till she's clean, she thinks, which should be just after the holidays; cause Nancy's gonna need something to get her through Christmas, maybe New Year's. By late afternoon she goes out to the mall and buys a paper turkey to show her husband when he comes home.

She's still a little fuzzy from her after-dinner blitz and when her husband starts to fuck her he wants to know how her tits got so bruised. Nancy sees the finger sized marks BJ left and thinks he must have squeezed them harder than she'd felt. Nancy kept her cool and told him she slept on her belly and hurt them that way. He fucked her doggie style which was worth the disgust and humiliation: at least she didn't have to see his face. She fantasized about handsome movie stars and baseball players and rock stars and mystery men with no names and her sister's husband Neal who she always thought was hot. But the pig-like grunts coming from her husband shattered all her pictures. She felt his flabby thighs smacking against hers and his mild explosion too soon, and as he slid out and sat on the bed and turned on the tv, Nancy could've dropped dead and he wouldn't have noticed. She thought of masturbating but then thought of something better.

When she came back up he was still sitting on the bed and as she passed him he went to kiss her but she kept on moving. Lying in bed to the Wall Street Report, she thinks of her supply, of how she smoked more today than she normally does, and then she remembers that today was a cop-day. She always smokes more on the days she cops. Tomorrow she'll go back to her normal amount and everything else will work itself out and she won't have to see BJ for at least five more days. Then she fell off to sleep as the Dow Jones dropped two points.

They're having a parade today. But Lourdes Alverez won't be attending. Neither will her infant son. It's a shame since she's the guest of honor. They'll all be there: her crying husband and teenage daughter, mayoral hopefuls and drug crusaders, all of them Sharptoning their tongues for the cameras. Lourdes would have enjoyed it. She won't be enjoying anything anymore, not since three nights ago when Sammy taught her a lesson for calling the police to stop him from conducting his very profitable business in front of their home. He didn't mean for them to kill her, just to shoot through the window, as a scare, but bullets are funny that way. All in all the message was sent. Sure, her husband talks big now of how he's gonna fight them harder and meaner. He's gonna get a gun permit so he can kill them all legally, but Sammy knows that once the cameras are off and the hopefuls find a new crusade, and Herman finds himself sitting home alone with his teenage daughter with no one to cook or clean or talk to or love, exhausted from his job and behind on his bills, he'll find another way to spend his time.

The parade's about to begin. Fire the rockets and enjoy the show...

Willy woke up with a roach on his face, crawling across his eye. He picked it off and pinged it out the open glassless window. He checked himself all over and seeing that nothing crawled up his nose or in his ears he got up from the floor and kicked his blanket under the bed. Mommy was still out from last night and Susie sat in the middle of the bed holding a dirty can filled with water. Next to her sat an empty box of saltines and when she asked Willy if he was hungry cause she saved him the last four, he told her to eat them and she did, then sipped from the can. Willy looked from the window down the street, grayer than usual, and everybody was hanging out on the stoop waiting for night to come. Susie asked where mommy was and Willy told her probably in hell and Susie told him that wasn't very nice.

He turned back and saw his sister picking the scattered crumbs from the blanket and licking them from her fingertips, then told her he'd get her something to eat.

The hallways reeked of pine-sol and the floors were glazed with dirty water and as Willy walked through he could feel a cold wet spot seeping through the hole in his sneaker. Good thing he wasn't wearing any socks. The lobby guards were throwing out Pukin' Mario with his garbage bag of cans but Mario was struggling to stay and as they dragged him out the door it looked like he was going to the electric chair. They tossed him in the gutter as everybody cheered and clapped and Mario jumped to his feet and shoved his fingers down his throat and tried to puke on Camille till she kicked him in the balls. Willy watched Mario stumble down the street with his bag over his shoulder like Santa Claus, then he headed east to Broadway to grub some change. By the time it started raining he had enough for two egg mcmuffs and some fries but when he got back to the room Susie was gone. He ate the fries and left the food under the blanket to keep warm. He checked his arms and shoulders and saw most of the welts had gone down. He hung his blanket from the rusted nails over the window to keep the rain from coming in, then went out front and asked Sizemore where his sister had gone. Sizemore didn't know. He sat on the stoop with the others and watched people splashing through puddles with newspapers and umbrellas over their heads and Rappin' Dave was trying to light a cigarette but it was completely soaked. Sizemore lit a joint and passed it to Willy who toked and choked till Sizemore told him to chill. The cops drove past but kept on going. Willy stared at the twitching images in a puddle near his foot, imagined he was a raindrop in this puddle of a world with everybody all stuck together just waiting for the sun to come out so they can dry up and disappear. From the corner came this little black stump of a thing walking down and the tiny bare feet sticking through the bottom told him it was her. As she got closer he saw her smiling face through the hole and asked where the fuck she'd been and what's with the trash bag. She told him she found it in the garbage and don't it make a great raincoat. He ripped the bag off her body and pulled her inside and told her if mommy came back and found her gone she'd be pissed as shit. He took her up to the room, gave her the food and ate the one she didn't want. From down in the street they heard screaming and yelling and Susie ran to the window. She stood on her toes to see Pukin' Mario trying to get back into the hotel and the guards were pushing and kicking and Willy couldn't believe how anybody'd be fighting to get in when they should be fighting to get out. Looking at his sister's wet and stringy hair, he told her that bag didn't make such a good raincoat, then he playfully pushed her down on the bed and dried her hair with the pillow. He pulled up his shirt and laid down on his belly and told her to draw pictures on his back with her fingers. As she did he tried to guess what they were. At four-thirty mommy stumbled in with big and bloodshot eyes. It looked like she didn't get any sleep. When Susie asked her where she'd been she said out. Willy pulled his blanket from the window and squeezed the water out on the floor while mommy yelled at him for making a mess. She asked Susie if she ate today and Susie told her about the egg mcmuffs. Willy went to the door and when mommy asked where he's going he told her out. On his way down he saw Chas on his way up and Willy hugged the wall as they brushed past each other without a word. Willy stopped outside Melody's door and listened for a minute but it sounded real quiet inside so he went out to the stoop and hung out with Sizemore who lit another joint. Willy didn't choke so much this time. Friendly-Frank-Who-Hates-The-World came by and asked for a toke but Sizemore told him to toke his dick and Frankie told him if he wasn't so friendly he would've kicked his fucking ass. He pulled out a tv antenna and asked if they wanted to buy it for fifty cents. When they said no he changed it to twenty-five. Sizemore told him to go to the playground and show the kids his fifteen-inch cock for a dime but Frankie said they've seen it already and nobody will pay anymore. Melody stepped out in her dirty baggy jeans with a rope for a belt and Willy tried not to look too happy. Sizemore offered her the joint and she toked without coughing then handed it to Willy who did. Willy told her he didn't hear anything outside her door and she said they were all crashed out. She asked for a cigarette but nobody had one so Willy said he'd buy one up the corner. He bought two loosey's with his last quarter and handing one to Melody she told him she'd pay him back tomorrow. Willy saw two empty cans in the gutter and took them, smiling at Melody, then they went back to the corner and bought two bazookas, the sweet pink kind. Melody had to stay near the hotel and Willy didn't ask why. The stoop was filling up as people stepped out and Willy and Melody hung out blowing bubbles and popping them with their fingers. Everytime Melody yelled "changes" they would switch gum and Willy thought this was the next best thing to kissing. The sun went down and her mother called from the window. Willy said he was going in too so they might as well go up together. He watched her disappear into her room then went on up to his own but it was empty.

Back on the street Chas stood off to the side as

mommy begged for some loose change to feed her little girl. Susie held her hand and together with pathetic hungry faces they blocked the sidewalk. Chas got pissed as most people just brushed past. A lady in a long green coat stopped and looking at Susie started to ask questions but mommy pulled her away and when the lady followed, Chas stepped up and told her to mind her own fucking business. The lady threatened to call the cops and the child welfare board but Chas told her to call an ambulance cause she was gonna need it. Mommy stepped over and said to Chas let's go home but Chas told her to shut her fucking mouth then tells the lady if she's so concerned about the girl why don't she give them some money to feed her. The lady turned to flag a cop and they all took off.

Up in their room mommy heats a can of stew on the hot plate and if the manager catches them cooking in the room again he's gonna throw their asses out into the street. Chas fries his brain out the window and mommy begs for a hit but he tells her to fuck off. Susie stirs the stew but the can tips over and mommy pulls her arm and curses about the wasted food and Chas looks over and says now it's all for him but after taking one bite he plops it down and tells them to choke on it.

The working girls stroll by the stoop and Sizemore tells Willy that he fucked Betty McBain last night in the stairway but Willy doesn't believe him cause Betty's old enough to be his mother. At that moment, Willy's mother steps out with Chas behind and she tells him to keep an eye on Susie and to make sure she stays in the room. She follows Chas down the street. Later Sizemore and Willy grub the theater crowd on 48th. In their minks and jewelry and suits and limos, Willy wonders what could be going on in these theaters cause these people don't seem real to him. They wait in front of the deli and seeing Friendly-Frank-Who-Hates-The-World they ask him to buy them beer and he says only if they give him two of the cans. Sizemore says they'll give him one but two cans wind up missing from the bag. Two cans each is enough to get drunk on and they go to Ninth to watch the girls. Melody stands in her pretty blue dress, her make-up thick, talking to the subhuman cretins and skells that make up her friends, and Willy feels this shiver down his back cause he thinks he's in love. At least as in love as a ten year old can be. Melody turns and sees him standing there and gives him a wink but he doesn't go over cause her mother warned him to keep the fuck away from her daughter. And though she's only twelve and has a list of steady clients, Melody if she were white she'd probably be rich by now.

On the way up the stairs Willy steps through the thick minty smoke and Rappin' Dave sits in the hallway launching rockets with Betty McBain who asks him what he's doing later and Rappin' Dave chuckles when Willy says he doesn't know. In the room Susie sits on the windowsill with one leg hanging out and Willy scares the hell out of her when he grabs her and pulls her inside. She starts crying as Willy yells what the hell are you trying to do and she says she was just watching below but he tells her to stay the fuck inside. She sits on the bed with an angry pout and Willy tells her to come over and he lifts her up to the sill but makes her keep her legs inside the room. They watch the traffic and the creeps down below. There's a scuffle in the hall and when Susie moves to open the door Willy grabs her arm and tells her not to. Later, Willy wakes to the sound of mommy and Chas coming in and they're both fucked out of their faces, laughing and fooling around and Chas is all over her groping and feeling and she's giggling and licking and Willy knew it was time to go into the hall. Susie slept with her face under the blanket and mommy told Willy to be careful as he lifted her out and laid her on the hallway floor. Susie rolled over and opened her eyes and didn't know where she was at first. Then she leaned against the wall next to her brother and listened to the squeaking and groaning from inside. Willy pulled up his shirt and told her to draw pictures on his back but she said she was tired, so she lay down on the floor with her hands folded under her face and tried to sleep.

The next morning Chas had them up early and mommy was groggy and told him she needed a hit to get herself going but Chas said he'd hit her good if she didn't snap out of it. He took her and Susie out onto Broadway and watched as they begged for change. Willy sat in the hall outside Melody's door and at the first sound of movement he was gonna run by screaming for no reason. He waited an hour then went out to the stoop and everybody was buzzing about how Pukin' Mario was arrested this morning by the cops and as they put him in their car he puked and they beat him up. At twelve Melody came out and Willy said to let's go get some lunch but neither of them had any money. Melody told him to wait outside as she went in and while waiting there he considered grabbing the bag of cans from a hunched-over bag-lady's cart when Melody came out with five bucks. They went to Popeye's and Willy chucked the bones of greaseball chicken legs on the floor till Melody told him to pick them up and as he did she threw them back down and they laughed. A Popeye-guy in his grease-stained life came by and told them to get the fuck out. Willy told him to eat shit but Melody told him to eat the chicken instead, and out on the street they had a good laugh. Melody's face was smooth chocolate in the sun and with her big round eyes Willy wanted to do something to her but he wasn't sure what. They hung out on the stoop and Pigtail Peggy played music from her box as Melody and Morris danced. Willy and Sizemore sat there with smiles on their faces. Chas and mommy came back with Susie who complained that she was tired and her legs hurt and Chas told mommy to get her the fuck inside. Chas stayed out and took the joint as Sizemore offered a toke. He asked Willy how much he grubbed today and when Willy said nothing Chas got real pissed and called him a fucking shithead waste of a life, then he cracked him one in the back of the head and as Melody stopped dancing Willy felt real small. Chas stormed inside and Willy followed without saying goodbye to Melody. Chas was counting money up in the room and figuring how much to spend on dinner when Willy stepped in. Chas told him he can eat his fucking toenails cause he's not getting any tonight, and mommy said he has to eat something even if it's just a plain hamburger but Chas told her if he doesn't work he doesn't eat and he won't hear backtalk or else she's not getting high, so mommy shut her mouth and gave Willy a cautious look. Chas started mumbling about how mommy lets too many people pass without paying and she doesn't try hard enough. He tells her she has to shove Susie right in their faces and they should try to look sadder and hungrier, but Willy sat on the edge of the bed and told him they couldn't look any sadder or hungrier. Chas flipped out and grabbed Willy and threw him against the wall and popped his face with an open hand and punched him in the stomach and Willy fell to the floor choking for air. Chas must've really had a bug up his ass tonight cause he started cursing mommy and saying how he hates her and her goddamn fucking kids and if she were even halfway decent-looking she could be out turning tricks. Mommy screamed that her welfare checks keep coming and he doesn't seem to mind when they do and Chas screams at her for being in this shithole of a situation and it's costing two-fucking-thousand dollars a month to stay here and that's money better spent on rockets. As mommy tries to say something else Chas pops her in the mouth. Susie runs over to the bed and sits next to Willy on the floor as Chas beats the shit out of their mother. They watch her flail on the floor as Chas punches her face and pulls her hair and bangs her head. When she tries to kick him he gives her a dozen pounding-charlie-horses till she rolls over and cries in her arms. Willy and Susie have no expression, they stare down at their feet. Chas turns on Willy next, screaming for him to make a move or try something so he can kill him and ditch his fucking body where it will never be found, and seeing the look in his eyes Willy knew that he meant it. Chas storms out. Willy and Susie hear their mother choking and sobbing on the floor. She lifts herself to the bed and Susie turns to look but Willy twists her head back. Not soon enough though, cause mommy cries that this is all Willy's fault and how his father was a fucking worthless piece of shit and Chas was never like this before but it's the pressure of having to care for two worthless kids and if she had it to do over again she would've aborted them both. Susie looked at Willy and he could see from her face that she didn't know what that meant.

Melody's working again tonight cause her mother needs her rockets. She stands there keeping watch to make sure everybody pays their due. Willy watches from behind the cars and Melody glances over like it's a secret game between them. But after watching her get into some of the cars and the look on her face when she gets out, Willy sneaks back to the hotel and hangs out on the stoop with Sizemore and Roberto the Guard. Sizemore was toking a joint and Roberto the Guard didn't tell him to put it out. That's when Willy knew Roberto was cool.

Betty McBain is hanging out in the lobby. She follows Willy half-way up the first flight and touches him from behind. She smiles when he turns around, and tells him she wants to show him something and it'll be something that he'll like. Willy is a

little tense cause Betty always gives him the creeps.
She leads him by the hand up the stairs past his
floor to the top where there's a small room off to
the side. She pulls off her blouse and Willy just
stares at her tits and the firm nipples pointing at
him like fingers. Betty takes his hand and makes
him touch them. They felt cold. She pulled his head
towards her and told him to suck. She kissed him on
the lips and stuck in her tongue and he could taste
the minty-burnt-out smell that mommy always has.
Betty slid off her skirt and stood there in frilly
string panties and garter belts across her thighs
and looking closer Willy could see her pussy coming through the cutout at the crotch. She knelt
down and undid his pants and pulled them to his
ankles and lying on her back on the cold tile floor
she asked him if he ever did this before and Willy
answered what. She giggled and spread her legs.
Willy stood there for a moment till Betty pulled him
in with her ankles. She took his cock in her hand
but it wasn't very hard and Willy couldn't see where
it would go anyway. Betty sat up and took him into
her mouth and Willy moaned and within seconds he
was hard but everytime Betty lay back down Willy
got soft again. Betty teased him and asked if he
liked boys and Willy wasn't so sure what that meant.
After the fourth try without success Betty told him
he was too young and that she'll see him in another

year. Willy pulled up his pants and went down the stairs and into the room where mommy and Chas were passed out on the bed while Susie sat on the floor drawing faces on a newspaper.

Willy heard screaming in the middle of the night and he was the only one awake cause when he whispered for Susie she didn't answer. The voice was crying and moaning for help and it sounded like some kind of really deep pain. It must've been a stabbing or something cause there was no gunshot. Willy would've heard it if there was. He hoped it wasn't somebody he knew. Staring up at the ceiling he said a prayer to whoever was up there just in case.

Willy woke up screaming as Chas stepped on his hand getting out of bed. Chas told him to stay closer to the window and don't lie near the edge of the bed if he doesn't want to get stepped on. Mommy was out cold and Chas had to sit her up before she would wake. He took the last two bagels from the night before and broke them in half and threw the pieces on the bed for Willy and Susie.

Melody came out on the stoop and said she's not working tonight cause she started bleeding so her mother gave her the night off. She and Willy sat on the stoop smoking cigarettes, watching the parade of freaks. Willy asked her why he always chokes smoking Sizemore's weed when he can smoke cigarettes without choking. Melody tells him that Size-more smokes the cheapest dirt-weed around. She says she'll cop something good today cause she snuck a twenty dollar tip from last night into her panties. They go down to Playland and Melody gives Willy four quarters and as he plays Defender and gets killed every time, she looks for somebody she knows. She approaches a guy as black as tar wearing a purple-hooded sweatshirt and he smiles when he sees her. He holds out his middle finger which she pinches in her teeth. Willy hears himself explode and looks down at the screen to see himself disintegrate into space. Melody comes over and says let's go and as they leave Melody says they'll have to get a stem and for a second Willy thought she was talking about flowers.

Willy loved the crackling popple sound as Melody kept the match moving past the resin-blackened bowl. He watched the glow in her eyes as they got wide for a second. She gently blew the smoke in his face and he felt her soul come with it. She held the stem and Willy took it and sucked in deep as Melody lit the bottom and told him to breathe in slow. Two seconds later Willy was fucked out of his brain and he almost toppled over till Melody grabbed his shirt and giggled. Melody tells him this is why she works the street and Willy can almost understand it now. The cement gave under his feet and the world tilted sideways and Melody was laughing cause he was lying on his side. She came over and sat him up. Willy thought he was paralyzed and just sat there holding on to the ground. Melody dragged him over to the wall, the cool brick on his back stopped the spinning. They talked and fired into the night and neither one tried to stand up. The whole time Willy was dreaming that they were married and living in the country doing what normal people do and having things and food and being in love and passion but everytime he got up the nerve to say something to her about it, he chickened out. She told him how she doesn't feel threatened by him and how he doesn't want anything from her like everybody else and that's why she likes him. He realized then he's just a kid to her and nothing to nobody and all he does is make trouble for everyfuckingbody he comes in contact with so he really can't blame her for just wanting to be his friend. A chill swept across his body though it was hot outside. They sat on the stoop and every guy who passed by tried to hit on Melody and Willy sat there feeling kind of worthless. He wondered if it might be better to not know her at all than to know her like this. Would he miss her if she weren't there or would there be something else in her place? At sunrise they were still awake and alone together cause Sizemore was out like a light and Colleen went to get cigarettes. Melody sat close and touched his knee and said how it would be good to get away and maybe they could just take off one day and never come back and what's holding them here and who would even miss them or care cause she hates her fucking mother and doesn't want to work for her and wouldn't it be better for them both to just sneak away? And though Willy never thought about it before he told her that it would. When Colleen came back Melody went back to her side of the stoop and grubbed a cigarette.

Susie sat in the corner holding a pillow in front of her. Mommy stayed on the bed and kept her mouth shut, hoping he would light up soon, cause Chas stalked the room grunting like an animal and kicking anything in his way. The last thing he wanted to see was Willy coming through that door and when Willy did and asked what was wrong, Chas whirled around and told him they're all a bunch of fuck-faced bastards and nobody's carrying their weight and there's not enough for food or rockets and he's not gonna take it anymore and he's tired of sacrificing himself and from now on there's gonna be some changes. Willy didn't know who he was talking about. Till Chas popped his face. Clean. Right on the cheek. Willy fell down howling like his skull was cracked with a needle shooting right through the middle. His face was red and his stomach heaving and when he opened his eyes he thought he was blind. Susie ducked behind her pillow and pretended she was invisible. Mommy looked over at her boy rolling on the floor like his soul had been ripped out, then over to Chas launching a rocket. He said the kid was only faking cause he didn't hit him that hard and he's sorry and didn't mean it and it'll never happen again and as he passed her the bazooka, she took it and fired. Willy's face blew up like a balloon and it was puffy and purple and his jaw hurt like a bastard and the only time he spoke was to cry. He didn't leave the room for the next few days cause he was ashamed. Susie acted as if he wasn't even there. When he finally did come out the last person he wanted to see was Melody so he waited till dark then hung out with Sizemore on the stoop. Sizemore kept telling him that with his new fucked-up purple-battered face he could really grub some cash but Willy softly told him no. Yesterday when Chas told him to quit puffing up his face on purpose then raised his arm as if to hit, Willy started crying for no reason and Susie crawled under the bed. Then mommy told Chas to quit hitting the kids and he told her he didn't lay a hand on them. He and mommy sat facing the window and Chas made her suck his dick. Willy reached under the bed and pulled Susie out and took her into the hall. Sitting there in silence with the smell of the hall mixing with the smoke from the room, Willy wanted to get high, to blitz his fucking brains and go anywhere but here. His sister stared straight ahead as if she were hypnotized. He asked her to draw pictures on his back but she ignored him. He shook her but she still wouldn't talk. He yanked her hair and smacked her face and made her cry, then he jumped up and screamed now how do you like it cause he never beats the fucking shit out of you, does he? Storming out of the hall as Susie sat there bawling, Willy felt this heat inside, growing and burning and he didn't know what to do about it. He ran to the construction site and smashed windows, with each crash of broken glass he felt a little better. Melody stood on Ninth but Willy passed her by and fuck her mother if she says something cause she doesn't own the fucking streets. Willy stopped in front of the appliance store and watched tv, wondering why he was born and what the fuck gives with this world and who the fuck are these people on tv living like kings and queens with homes and cars and clothes and nobody really lives like that cause it's all just make-believe.

Sizemore had these tiny scab-like dots on his arm and when Willy asked what they were Sizemore told him pimples. Then Sizemore buttoned his sleeve and put a finger to his lips. Willy saw Chas, mommy and Susie grubbing on 46th and Chas was leaning against the wall as mommy and Susie did all the work. Seeing that look on Chas' face Willy wanted to shoot him dead. Instead he went to the deuce and stole a pretzel for lunch, then snuck into a kung fu movie. Afterwards he hung out in front of Peeptown but all he could see inside were the rows of books and booths. A black-skinned blonde on the corner was showing off her legs but her arm was in a cast and her face was kind of old and underneath the wig you could see the fro fighting through. The window of the surplus store was packed with knives and mace and pipes and cuffs and fake id's and chukka sticks and flying stars and bowie knives and looking through the window Willy thought he saw a rifle. He turned and was surrounded by three demanding his money. They didn't believe him so they ripped through his pockets and threw him to the ground. Willy stayed there till they left, thankful nobody popped his cheek.

They were sitting on the bed eating burgers when Willy came in. Mommy tossed him one and he sat on the floor watching his sister who still wouldn't look at him. Mommy and Chas were smiling at each other so they must've had a good day. Susie scraped her pickles off and put them on her napkin. Willy asked if he could have them and she held them out but turned her head. Chas got up and scooped the wrappers and told mommy he was going to the store. He told Willy to come with him and Willy got scared for a second, but stood up and went anyway. Going down the stairs Chas asked him how his face was and Willy told him okay. He said how sorry he was and how he didn't mean it, that he just lost his temper and went crazy for a minute and could Willy ever forgive him. Willy told him to forget it and Chas put his hand on Willy's shoulder as if he liked him, but Willy felt this chill inside cause Chas was like lit dynamite. Chas bought two packs of Camels and a six of beer at the deli and on the way home he told Willy the beer was for him. When they reached the stoop Chas asked Willy to do him a favor. He and mommy were going out for a few days and would he promise to watch out for Susie and keep her in the room till they get back. Willy asked where they were going but Chas snapped that it was none of his business. Then he softened a moment and said they were going to visit his brother in Newark. Heading back up the stairs Willy was hoping they would see Betty McBain so he could see how Chas deals with her, but they didn't. Mommy and Chas were excited and buzzing like flies as they put their clothes into paper bags. Susie watched from the windowsill. Mommy told them both to behave and that they'll be back on Wednesday and when Susie asked where they were going mommy told her out. Chas gave Willy ten bucks and told him to be careful with it and if he needed more to grub it from the street. They left and Susie looked at her brother for the first time in a week. She asked him what they should do but he said he couldn't see her cause she was invisible. She held her hand in front of her face and told him she wasn't anymore but he told her to see how she likes it. Then he lifted his shirt and lay on the bed and when Susie came over and drew pictures on his back, he tried to guess what they were. Later he took her out to the stoop with him and when she said she was hungry he bought her a crunch bar. Sizemore lit a joint and blew the smoke in Susie's face then passed it to Willy who did the same and Susie took a deep breath and said it smelt like burning flesh. Sizemore asked Willy if he had any money to cop. Susie looked over but didn't say anything. The moon was hidden by clouds and everything was quiet as Willy, Sizemore and Rappin' Dave watched the night dissolve. Susie napped on the cool cement steps; Willy thought he saw a UFO. Then he noticed Rappin' Dave staring at his sister and he didn't like the look of it, so he nudged her awake and took her up to the room. Reaching the door, she told him this was the latest she's ever stayed out. Willy tried to sleep in the bed but it was too soft so he went back to the floor. Bright and early the next morning Susie was tapping him awake cause she said her belly was talking to her. Willy sat up and wiped his face as Susie picked chips off the wall and flicked them out the window. Willy went out and came back with two buttered bagels and a pint of chocolate milk and so far they were doing good cause they still had seven bucks and a dime left.

Melody was beaten up last night and when they took her to the hospital her mother got arrested. Rappin' Dave was saying how she was sliced up along her tits but it wasn't as bad as it looked and the guy who did it drove off with a bloody front seat but Melody's mother got the plate number and gave it to the cops. The story made Willy shake all over and his legs became jelly and he couldn't imagine anybody wanting to hurt poor Melody. He waited all day on the stoop but Melody never came back. Nobody knew if she was still in the hospital or in jail with her mother.

Betty McBain came out when the sun went down. Everytime she looked at Willy she gave him a crooked smile. She told him not to worry cause Melody was taken upstate to Goshen where they would keep her away from her mother and all the other fucked up people. They'll get her off drugs and into God and by then she'll probably be a vegetable. This didn't sound so good to Willy, so he started asking where Goshen was and how could he get there and Betty told him to take a bus at the Port. She acted serious but laughed behind her teeth and the more Willy bought it the more desperate she made it sound. She told him that she was there when it happened and that Melody was calling his name and saying how much she needed him and where could he be and why did he leave her like this. Betty suggested he grub some money for the bus and when Willy asked her how much she told him about thirty. Willy decided to use Susie like mommy and Chas do, with her pathetic little face they could probably grub the money in an hour. When Susie asked why they were doing this Willy told her for a friend. A cop car slowed down and Willy didn't like the cops' faces so he grabbed Susie and they took off down the street. He only had twenty bucks but he wasn't gonna wait cause he had to get up there quick and take Melody away before something happens. Maybe they could hide out and get married and fry their brains and be together for the rest of their lives. First he had to ditch Susie. He held her hand as they grubbed their way to the hotel. Susie squeezed his hand real hard with her face looking down and her steps getting smaller and Willy hoped she wouldn't give him a hard time. He stopped at the deli and bought two Hersheys and a Kit-Kat. He asked if she wanted anything else and she told him to buy potato chips. With the open bag of chips she was now walking normally with Willy keeping two steps ahead. Betty McBain was gone when they got back and Willy wanted to ask her a few more questions so he went up to the top floor hallway but she wasn't there. He took Susie to the room and picked through a pile in the corner gathering all of his belongings: a shirt, a jacket, and a red rubber eraser shaped like a skull. Susie just sat on the bed and watched. He took out his money and put ten aside. He'll go as far as he can on seventeen, then grub at the next stop. Over on the bed Susie's pitiful little face ripped a hole through his guts. She cried and begged him to stay or at least take her with him and as much as he tried to explain, she wouldn't listen. He told her that she's better off without him cause all he does is make trouble and that's why Chas hits him and mommy hates him but Susie explained that if he wasn't around to get hit then maybe Chas will start on her. Willy told her that won't be happening. Then Susie said that Chas would be really mad when Willy came home but Willy told her that won't be happening either. She told him she would draw pictures on his back and as she tried to lift his shirt he pulled it down and told her to stay in the room till mommy gets back. He gave her the ten bucks and wiped her cheeks with his sleeve. With one last look he told her to behave, then went to the door. He couldn't look back, so he turned the knob and stepped into the hall. Stood there for a minute. Listening to his sister cry. Then he barrelled down the stairs and headed for the station.

USED CARS

There'll be no used cars sold today. Things have gotten too damn hot around here. Eat your spaghetti and take your gun off the table.

At nine yesterday evening Kevin Coogan of Bay Ridge, Brooklyn, was shot in the face in a grocery store on East Fifth after spraying beer at the owner Doo Kim Chang of 80th street. When the cops came they charged Chang with murder and took the unlicensed .45 caliber gun he kept in the store.

Twenty minutes later Mitchell Corona of Sutter in Queens was shot three times in the chest as he tried to resist a robbery attempt. If they were just gonna take his stuff that was cool but there was no way they were taking his wife's. As he died in the gutter she cried on his body and begged him to live.

Later at ten, Domingo Ferrara was sitting on his Bushwick stoop when a pack of noisy punks came by whooping and howling and when Domingo asked them to be quiet one of them pulled a gun and shot him in the guts. Now he's lying in the hospital and they're not so sure he's gonna make it.

An hour later Tommy Clark was fatally shot two blocks from his East New York home following a dispute over quantity.

At ten to twelve Gary Gaddone was found lying in the street outside his Staten Island home where he was shot once in the chest and once in the throat. There was a sock stuffed in his mouth and nobody knew what the fuck that meant.

At twelve-fifteen Willy Meyers of 194th was shot to death on 153rd when a guy jumped from a Caddie and screamed out his name then pumped eleven shots into him before driving away.

A nude woman in her twenties was found dead with her throat slashed in between two dumpsters at the supermarket on Amsterdam. Nobody knows who she is or where she's from but one of the neighbors thought she looked like Tina Turner.

At one-thirty the cops found the body of a man in the trunk of a stolen car parked in front of St. Adalbert's. A plastic bag covered his head and when they pulled it off, his face had been smashed with a blunt object.

Kenny Wilson died early this morning in police custody after he was arrested for kidnapping his girlfriend's six-year-old daughter. When he became violent in his holding cell on Foster he had to be subdued. Two and a half hours later he died at the hospital though no one could find any bruises.

At quarter to four they found Hector Burris, 14 years old, shot in the head at the Tilden Houses. Although he'd been missing for over a week the gunshot wound was fresh.

Two hours later, Farian Phillips was found beaten to death on East 105th and the cops are now looking for his brother Hansa, wanted on a weapons warrant. Three blocks away Carolyn Rogers was found dead in her car shot four times in the chest but the cops weren't looking for Hansa on that one.

At twenty after six, after opening the deli only ten minutes earlier, Larry Mason and his nineteen-year-old son TJ were shot to death during a four dollar robbery. Neither one of them put up a struggle. They were shot just standing there.

The headless mutilated body of a woman was found burning in a pile of trash in Jamaica, Queens, at seven-o-seven. The cops could tell from her arm that she was using. So far, they haven't found the head.

At ten-thirty this morning a crazed gunman burst into his ex-wife's apartment and shot her and his two daughters to death before killing himself. The cops say a court order had been in effect.

At eleven o'clock on the basketball courts, Bobby Crown was shot to death by a sniper while going for a layup. The gunman was not found.

At twelve noon the entire fucking world just stopped for a minute and said what the fuck's going on around here and what the fuck gives with all this shit and what's driving these fucking people so crazy.

At twelve-o-one Sally Pearson was shot dead in the crossfire from a drug dispute.

Marybeth Montell was proud of her gifts. For a man she was well endowed. Hard as wood and cold as clay and filled with who-knows-what, but they were there to set the snare and by then it was too late. Benny would cut you bad if you backed out. From standing cars the bobbing heads tap out their beats of jizz, while Marybeth who's out of breath rolls up her tattered sleeve.

It burns at first and numbs her arm before it explodes like a roman candle in the middle of her skull. A shot of class, champagne for the vein, and Benny always finds the right spot, knows exactly when to squeeze. She loves Benny. He's the only man who makes her cum, the only man who drives down Hershey Boulevard cause Marybeth is clean and gonna stay that way. She stands on the corner in alphabet Texas with the other girls—all corner boys in drag, some with tits—but none with Marybeth's talent. She's the queen. When she started wearing bags they all did, and now no one does a job without one unless they're too fucked up in the head to care. Blotch cream is a big seller off Houston.

Benny tells the guy from Queens that Marybeth's available and for the right price she'll suck him behind the Chinese restaurant. The guy from Queens says okay but not to use the rubber. But Marybeth slips it on and does him so he doesn't notice. She's a talent, that Marybeth—when Dominick O'Malley offered her fifty bucks to teach him how to do it Benny told him to get his scurvy ass the hell away from his wife. That Benny, she thought, always looking out for my best interests. No girl could find any better.

They met three years ago in a gallery off the Bowery, two doors from the Palace Hotel. This was before Marybeth had tits. Benny was copping rockets while Marybeth was there for her shot. She couldn't find her vein so Benny helped; when she passed out he took her home and put her to bed. She woke up pissed as shit and told him he had no fucking right to touch her or move her or take her to his place and that she wasn't doing anything with him so he'd better let her the fuck out. He agreed and she never left. They've been trying to get married for a year now but no one will perform the ceremony, not even that homo priest from St. Elizabeth. They exchanged wire rings and in their minds they're married. Marybeth does the cooking and cleaning and laundry and she finds joy in doing all the house-work and bullshit normal girls would say is fucked up. Between the money she makes and the money he steals they're doing alright with enough left over for rent.

After dinner he tells her she doesn't have to go out if she doesn't want to, but she wants to. He helps her wrap up the meatloaf and throw out the salad and he shoots up her shot. Then they go hand in hand off Houston. While Marybeth's doing a guy in the front seat, Benny stands nearby fingering his knife. Seeing her head through the window and imagining the sounds and the moaning and the stroking of hair, Benny feels helpless. He still can't get used to it. If only he was able to buy it for her... But shit, Marybeth's shooting a hundred a day and Benny knows he can't steal that much, not on a regular basis. He laughs at the thought of it.

Marybeth steps out of the car wiping her chin and he can't even look at her so he goes down the street and ignores her when she calls out his name. Good riddance, he thinks. He fires a hit and closes his eyes and swims through the night pushing stars out of his way. He sees different planets and the earth down below, and he wants to share it with someone cause alone these things don't mean as much, so he turns back to find Marybeth.

She was leaning against the wall and when he came near she turned away. He grabbed her shoulders and made her look at him and with his green eyes shooting charges he told her that it was a fucked up thing for him to leave her alone like that cause she's the most beautiful thing off Houston and he's sorry.

He kisses her on the lips and she gives him a smile.

Benny watched her do three more jobs then they both went over to Ridley's place. Ridley had money and didn't have to work so he just stayed home trying on different outfits. Benny noticed the moment he saw him that his tits were twice the size they were on Wednesday. Marybeth asked how it went and Ridley just giggled and said marvelous. He proudly pulled them out and told Benny to feel them but Marybeth warned be gentle cause they're probably still a little sore. Benny touched them and bounced them and lightly squeezed the nipples which felt like rocks. Ridley bent over and lifted his skirt and showed them his new puffed-out ass and Benny felt that too.

Inside the huge dark loft candles burned; art and statues, rugs and drapes and trinkets took up every

empty space. Benny shot their veins and fired hits
while Marybeth made Ridley into a whore. Benny
watched the Knicks on tv, even though he hates
sports. He chugged Chivas and the two girls planned
for Ridley's coming-out party now that he has real
tits. Ridley says he has to tell his mother and brothers but he isn't looking forward to it. Marybeth tells
him no matter what they'll think, he'll still have her
and Benny. Ridley and Marybeth make up a list of
what to buy and when Ridley asks if he should get
some ludes Marybeth says absolutely, then she
writes it down. When they finish the list Ridley and
Marybeth talk about art and books and films and
food and shit that Benny can't pronounce let alone
understand. Marybeth looks over at Benny nodding
out on the couch and wonders how the hell she got
stuck with such a mental midget.

The Stones came on the radio singing sympathy
for the devil and Marybeth and Ridley got up to
dance. Benny opened his eyes and seeing them
dance real close he perked up but didn't make a
sound. He was getting excited, and what would
really turn him on is if Ridley would go down on his
wife. But there'd be no lesbian encounters with
Marybeth cause in that way she was straight, so
Benny just watched and dreamed.

"What did you think of Ridley's tits?" she asked
him on the walk home.

"I told him what I thought."

"But what did you *really* think?"

"I thought they were alright."

"But did you think they were better than mine?"

"Better than your what?"

"Tits! My tits. What the hell are we talking about!?"

"I don't know."

"Well, what did you think? I mean, cause hers are new and mine are older. Is there any difference in the softness?"

"No, I mean, yeah, yours are much softer, and better shaped too. You know that. I love your tits." After a pause, "Why, what did you think of them?"

"I thought they did a real nice job," she said slightly distracted. "They can hide the scar so much better now, you couldn't even see it on her. That's what I mean, do you think I should get mine redone?"

"Oh comon Marybeth. Don't start this shit again, your tits are perfect. Believe me, you make a great girl."

"Yeah?" she says, looking for reassurance.

"Look, you're my wife and I'm not complaining am I? So leave it at that."

Marybeth took his hand and they went home and got real fucked up. The next morning he couldn't wake her and her eyes were rolled up in her head.

Her breathing was slow and deep, he got real scared for a minute. He sprinkled some cold water on her face and she opened her eyes and asked what planet she was on. He yelled that she scared the shit out of him and how one of these days he's gonna find her dead and how much more of this shit does she expect him to take. He called her a fucking lazy drugaddict bitch. Marybeth just sat up and rubbed her baggy eyes, pulled on her nightie, and asked Benny what kind of eggs he wanted for breakfast. She passed him to get to the bathroom and in the sterile light of day, he noticed how much she really looked like a man. Even with her giant tits and tiny waist and perfect ass and shapely legs there was still something not right about it. Whatever it was, Benny hoped that she'd correct it in the bathroom. But she didn't. She stepped over to the side of the bed, picked up the dirty tissues and put them in the basket, complaining that Benny never puts the dirty tissues where they belong. Benny tells her it's her shit and she should be responsible but Marybeth calls him an animal. They start snapping and throwing names at each other but after a minute they both begin to laugh.

Marybeth cooks him eggs over easy and makes him coffee and he grabs her ass at the table and they kiss and while Benny fires the bazooka, Marybeth cooks her fix. Benny shoots it and tells her she'll have to find a new vein soon cause this one's almost dead. She slumps to the table with her head laying sideways, drool hangs from her mouth and she moans like she's having sex. Benny lights another. Blitzed out of his face he wants to fuck her bad but she's unconscious. How could they be so different in their drugs, he wonders. When he's up she's down and it's a miracle they ever get together at all. But seeing her like this he thinks she's the most gorgeous thing he's ever seen and he goes over and kneels near her face and starts licking the drool from her lips. She sticks out her tongue and he sucks it then rubs his hand along her thigh. With her eyes all aflutter he lifts her up and carries her into the bedroom. He imagines from the back it looks like Gone With The Wind. He lays her down, opens her gown and rubs her tits and strokes the scar just under the mound. He licks her nipples and sucks her neck and mounts her face then rolls her over and fucks her. After wiping himself clean he drops the tissue in the basket, then lies on his side and runs his fingers through her thin silky curls. He touches her cheek and feels the stubble like sand cause she didn't shave yet and no matter how many pills she takes the stubs keep coming back. But as long as she's his who gives a shit if they both have cocks cause that's nature's fault not his. He tried it the normal way with his first wife and she fucked him over good with her lying and cheating and lying and it's a miracle he didn't poke her fucking eyes out with a tire iron. He goes to the kitchen window and launches another rocket. Staring down at the pavement below he wonders what the drop would feel like. Would it be like blasting and would he feel the impact? He pictured Marybeth running out and crying over his crumpled body and then at his funeral she'd jump on the coffin and scream, "Benny, please don't leave me," and how many men can say they have a woman like that in their lives.

On the corner Benny leaned against the wall and watched his wife with the others. They giggled and gossiped and Marybeth was the center of attention. Everytime a car pulled over they surrounded it and one would get inside. A Monte Carlo stopped at the light, the windows came down and the back-seat boys started calling Marybeth and her friends a bunch of homo-faggot AIDS-infesters and why don't they go to an island somewhere and die slow and painful deaths. Before the light turned green Marybeth chased after the car chucking bottles and cursing them out but they screeched away in laughter. Marybeth would've killed them if she could. Benny took her hand and told her to relax that it was just a bunch of assholes from Jersey out in their father's car, but she was real upset about it. Resting her head on his shoulder she started crying, cause

Marybeth already lost too many friends, and it wasn't funny and it wasn't something she was gonna ignore and she wished that every straight person who took delight in the homo-plague hysteria could live just one day in the ravaged body of poor Florentine. Benny took her home and shot her up and counted her scores—over two hundred bucks. He put her to bed and turned on the set and watched the Reverend Dickhead O'Jesus call him a sinner.

Marybeth woke up alone in bed and called for Benny but there was no answer. The place was empty. Wiping the sun from her face she got up and went inside and took her pills and shaved her legs and took a bath with oil. She dressed in a free-flow short-blue springtime dress, combed her curly brown hair and let it fall down her back. After making the bed and cleaning the apartment she went into the kitchen to find the money jar empty. Checking her stash there was only enough left for today. She took the glass needle Benny used last night and put it in a pot of water mixed with alcohol and waited for it to boil. She cleaned her works with cotton swabs and put it away. Benny came back two hours later. He pulled out a plastic pencil pouch and dumped it on the table where three days of happiness rolled out. Marybeth smiled. He pulled out six brand new plastic needles still wrapped in their cellophane and her eyes went wide with delight. Fresh needles were hard to get. They fried their brains and fixed their veins and it was special when Benny fixed cause he didn't fix too often; he was the only one she'd ever share a needle with. They spent the day in bed watching visions on the ceiling and when Marybeth went down on him he was tempted to suck her back but Benny's a pitcher not a catcher.

Benny wakes to JR's knocking and stumbles out of bed while Marybeth snores into the pillow. He lets him in, telling him to be quiet cause his wife's asleep. He chucks him a Pabst and lights a hit. JR tells him about this place he's staked out where they've got all kinds of expensive shit: big tv's and stereos and furniture and paintings. Benny points out that they can't carry that kind of shit out the window, but JR tells him if people got that kind of shit in their place it only stands to reason that they got money and jewelry and who knows what other goodies. It's been a month since the last job and Benny needed the money so he said alright let's do it. JR asks to use the bathroom and though Benny didn't want to say no he didn't want to say yes cause JR smelt like a fucking sewer. Marybeth wakes up while JR's in the bathroom and looking at Benny she opens the window. Benny asks her why she didn't sleep a little longer and Marybeth says who could sleep through JR's stench. He tells her that he's doing a job tonight and that she has to stay home till he gets back. As JR steps out of the bathroom Marybeth sprays Lysol; JR waves the cloud from his face and sits at the table. Marybeth asks him if he wants something to eat and JR says what do you got and Marybeth opens the fridge and says beer, food and soap. Benny chuckles but JR didn't know why. Marybeth made him a sandwich and Benny caught him sneaking a look at Marybeth's ass as she stood at the counter in her short pink robe. She went inside and closed the door while Benny and JR continued to smoke and plan their job. After ten minutes Marybeth called Benny into the room where she was cooking her fix. Benny unwrapped one of the brand new needles and seeing the bubbling hunk of saliva, told her it was too much but Marybeth said if she's gonna be home all night alone she's gonna be fixed just right. Benny cursed how one of these days he's gonna kill her with too much and it's gonna be all his fault and why doesn't she get a fucking grip on herself and go back to rockets. Nonetheless he filled the needle and when she asked him when he'd be leaving he said in a couple hours.

"Be careful, alright?" she said with concern. Then glancing at the door, "Watch it with him, he's a nut."

"I'll be fine, the place is empty, they're out of town."

"Alright, just be careful, that's all."

"I will be."

"Listen, if you're not back by the time I crash, I'm gonna go to Ridley's, okay? Meet me there, I'll make you dinner."

"How you gonna get there?"

"I'll walk."

"I don't want you walking there alone at night."

"I'll be alright."

"No you won't, it's dangerous."

"It is not."

"For *you* it is. I don't want you to go."

"Then I'll take a cab."

"Look, you're not going."

"Yes I am."

"Why don't you just wait for me here?"

"Because I don't want to sit home alone. If I have to do that I'd rather be working."

"Alright, take a fucking cab then. Just don't walk. And don't let me catch you working tonight."

"I won't...daddy." She gives him a smirk and he playfully pushes her down on the bed and lifts her left foot, pulling apart her middle toes. He finds a smooth tiny vein and hits it the first try. He draws out a full tube of blood and looking into Marybeth's eyes he shoots the whole thing like a rifle. Marybeth clutches the sheets and moans—JR must've thought they were having sex. Benny puts the works away and told her to be good and kissed her lips and watching from the bedroom doorway, her eyes glazed like crystal.

Ridley was confused over what name to take cause now that he was coming out, he had to change his name. While Benny stuffed his face on a huge plate of lasagne, Marybeth helped Ridley go through names. They searched through books and films and threw out dozens of fancy names from history and Benny couldn't imagine how they remember all this shit. Ridley gave Benny an eight to cook with ether and he mixed it in the bathroom because of the candles all over the place. They fried their brains and thought of names and out of nowhere Benny said how about Gabrielle. Ridley looked at Marybeth and after thinking about it for a second Marybeth nodded that it was okay. So Ridley became Gabrielle. Marybeth asked Benny how he thought of that name and he said it just came to him cause he didn't want to tell her he saw it on the back of a bus. Ridley pranced around in a French dress while Marybeth announced that on ramp 15 Gabrielle was modeling the latest spring fashion. Benny sat there smiling cause it was like watching two young girls at a pajama party. Marybeth looked at him with her eyes twinkling in the dark glow of the candles; when she smiled and her lips curved to one side it made him melt inside. He glanced towards the door and she softly nodded. Before they left she told Ridley she would get him a date for the party, one of her clients, a gentleman she said, very nice.

"Who's this guy that's so nice," Benny asked on the walk home. Marybeth looked at him with a wry smile cause she liked when he was jealous.

"Oh, just a client."

"Yeah I know that, but who is he? I want names."

"His name's Edgar Portman, he's an accountant."

"Do I know him?"

"I don't believe you've been introduced."

"That's not what I mean."

"Well, you've seen him I'm sure. He drives the dark blue Volvo station wagon."

"That guy?!" Benny exclaims. "He looks like a turtle!"

"Oh he does not. And he'd be perfect for Ridley; he's shy, not bossy, Ridley would be in total control the whole evening."

"Sure, all he'd have to do is flip little Edgar on his shell and he'd never get up."

"Oh be quiet."

Four guys hang out in front of the deli drinking and smoking as Benny and Marybeth pass. The guys goof on them, call them fags and freaks and threaten to rape Marybeth and cut off her dick. Marybeth squeezes Benny's arm as they keep walking; a bottle smashes right behind them. Benny reaches for his knife but Marybeth whispers to just keep going, so he does. They speed up their pace and hear sneakers following and without looking behind Benny sneaks his knife out, clicks it open. Another bottle smashes inches away and Marybeth's legs get sprayed with glass. In a flash Benny whirls around waving his blade and cursing them out, calling them limp-dick pieces of shit. As they attack, Benny slices two across the chest then screams for Marybeth to run but she pulls out a can of mace and starts spraying and kicking and Benny gets cracked over the head with a bottle. Somebody pulls a gun and fires, hitting the window of a parked car. Benny and Marybeth take off for their lives down the street. Benny pulls her into the first alley they pass, through the back yards and playground till they're alone. He's bleeding real bad and after dabbing it with a hankie and seeing the size of the gash, Marybeth takes him to the hospital. In the emergency room with the junkies and drunks she feels like some kind of creature from space. She wonders what the fuck she's doing here at five in the morning with a crack-head simpleton who's idea of a good time is frying his brain and feeding his face and staring at paint chips on the ceiling.

One of these days he's liable to get her killed with his goddamn fucking temper. One slimy drunk lying on the floor choked himself awake and seeing Marybeth for the first time, started calling for a surgeon. Benny came out with his head bandaged and seventeen stitches holding it together. As they left, the slimy drunk yelled for them both to go back to the circus and everybody laughed including the nurses. Marybeth waved for a cab but Benny told her he wanted to walk, and they started down the street without a word.

"I'm sorry," he said.

"You're the one with the stitches," she answered without looking over.

"I'm sorry for tonight. And for tomorrow. I'm sorry for the fucking world...And I guess I'm sorry that you're stuck with me." She looked at him and now he was the one looking away.

"Marybeth, I know what I am. Don't think for a second that I don't, cause I do. When I hear you and Ridley talking, even you and some of the girls, the things youse are able to talk about...I know that being with me must be like being in kindergarten. I look in the mirror, and I wonder what the fuck you're doing with me sometimes. I know that you do too. And I wait for the day when you find somebody else, cause eventually that's gonna happen. So don't worry, cause when it's over with us..."

His voice trailed off and he looked down at his feet. After a moment of feeling alone he stopped and turned around. Marybeth stood there watching him. And in that second maybe she realized something, that in some ways Benny's real smart. Maybe what he lacks in schooling, he makes up for in heart. Cause at the heart of it all he did love her, and no matter what she was, man, woman, creature-from-space, whatever, he loved her for it. How many women can say they have a man like that in their lives? She hugged him tight and when he asked why she was crying she told him to shut up. She took his hand and they walked home as the sun came up over the water.

Marybeth had been in the bathroom for hours and Benny was starting to get pissed. The door finally opened, she stepped out and Benny almost choked when he saw her. Wearing a short black dress with a flower design, her hair puffed up and trailing down her back like a cape, her lips soft crimson, her lashes and liner, blush and perfume, made her into a foxy hot bitch he wanted to fuck now and not later. She fixed his collar and when he went to kiss her she told him to watch her make-up. She took a silk scarf and wrapped it around his head like a turban and when he told her he was no terrorist, she told him it covers the bandage and to leave it on. He fixed her veins with half a dose and they left together.

The party was rocking and people were talking and smoking and drinking and Marybeth kept things moving along. When skinny frail Edgar came in with his wire rims, bow tie and tight little suit, Marybeth introduced him to Gabrielle then left them alone. All the homos off Houston were there: Jackie and Toni and April and Sharon toking around the multi-bong while Carli's boyfriend Raymond was frying his brain in the kitchen with Benny. Marybeth came in to get some sour cream and Benny asked how she was doing and told her to let him know when she wants another shot—they'll do it in the bathroom. Gabrielle stumbled in and said that she really liked Edgar and is there any more champagne. JR cruised through the room and stopped at every tray of food to glom. When Marybeth came out with a tray of mushrooms he was on it like a disease, and through the dozens of lit scented candles, she could still smell his stench so she gave him the tray and went to open a window. Janet J started singing about diamonds and Love Don't Come For Free and Rosine turned it up and everybody started dancing. Benny sat in the corner with a boner down his leg. He noticed that Edgar seemed to be having a good time. Marybeth came dancing through the crowd and seeing her husband with a bulge in his pants, she told him to put that thing away, then gently pinched it with her fingertips. Across the room Domino and Bela were arguing skin-popping versus main-lining and when they asked Edgar what he thought, he said he didn't know. Carmine from Cuba sat next to Benny and chugging his Bud asked Benny if he'd ever seen so many queers in one place at the same time before. Benny didn't know what to say to that. Carmine explained that he and Benny weren't really queer cause their wives are just like real women in that they dress up and have smooth soft skin and shapely bodies and this summer Rachel's having her change-op and then she'll be the true woman that she is inside. Benny told him that love doesn't know the difference. But Carmine told him that he hates queers and the only reason he's here is cause the woman he loves was born with a cock. Benny calls him an idiot and Carmine jumps up and says he thought Benny was a man but now he can see that he's just as queer as all the other fruitcakes. Benny says thank you and Carmine can't respond so he goes out the fire escape. In the bedroom doorway Ridley lets Roxanne feel her tits and when she starts comparing them to her own, they both look over at Wanda cause hers are still falsies. Dana, Layla and Rosemarie sat on the couch and between the three of them they barely made up one whole person, and Layla and

Rosemarie used to be fat. They sip their juice and everybody's acting polite but a little too much so. Benny wonders if this is how they're all gonna wind up and maybe it really is the fucking plague all over again and maybe there's no escape cause they don't even know what the fuck it is or how to stop it and everybody's just pissing in the dark and as long as they don't think they got it, they're in no rush.

Elton sang about tiny dancers and through the crowd Marybeth reached for Benny's hand and lead him into the middle of the room where she turned to face him and they danced. Benny felt her breath on his neck and her gentle kisses and her tongue and he started breathing hard and whispering let's go in the bedroom. Marybeth gave him a drunken smile and told him to be patient. But everytime she felt his cock go down she gave him another lick and Benny quietly threatened to fuck her good when they got home.

Suddenly there's a scream and commotion and everybody crowds into the hallway outside the bathroom. Marybeth and Benny cut through the crowd to see Monique lying on the floor where she dropped like dead weight from standing a moment ago. Marybeth sat her against the wall and patted her cheeks with cold water and after a few moans and groans and a heave of saliva Monique opened her eyes and asked what the fuss was about. Everybody let out a laugh including Ridley who wasn't too convincing. Monique crawled into the bathroom to puke up her life and they all went back to whatever they were doing. Marybeth pulled Benny into the bathroom for a fix. He took the works out of his pocket while watching Monique puke in the bowl. She asked for a hit but Marybeth told her she's crazy. Benny loaded the tube with not too much as Marybeth sat on the tub pulling down her nylons. Monique puked out a burst then said she'd never heard of shooting your toes and Benny told her a vein's a vein. Marybeth slumped down in the tub with her feet in the air as Benny launched a rocket and passed it to Monique, who puked in between tokes.

At quarter past four after everybody left, Marybeth and Benny put Ridley to bed. They looked around at the mess and decided to clean it tomorrow.

Outside, Marybeth looks for a cab but Benny tells her no cab'll come by at this hour; he starts walking but she doesn't follow. He turns around and says let's go but she tells him she doesn't feel like getting shot at tonight. He yells that it wasn't his fault and he was only trying to protect her but she tells him if he really wants to protect her he should buy her a bullet-proof vest. Benny calls her a fucking bitch and Marybeth says she's taking the train. She turns and walks away leaving Benny watching and wanting to give her one good pop in the face. She reaches halfway to the corner before he jogs after her, they both go down the stairs together. Marybeth takes two tokens from her purse and hands him one before pushing through the turnstile. She turns back to see Benny hopping over with a grin cause he knows she hates that. They stroll to the end of the platform.

"I was really surprised at Edgar tonight," she says out of nowhere. "That wasn't right."

"Why? What was wrong about it?"

"He was there as Rid—Gabrielle's date, he should have stayed with her."

"Well she should'a stayed conscious, that wasn't Edgar's fault."

"Still, he had no right to be fooling around with Dooli."

"I think if your date gets fucked up and passes out that gives you the right to fuck any bitch that's still awake."

"That's crude, and you're an animal! You always take the man's side anyway."

"Yeah, cause I'm a man!"

"A real man doesn't need to justify the acts of an asshole."

"Look, if Ridley wanted Edgar so bad, he shouldn't have gotten so fucked up, that's all I'm saying."

"And her name is Gabrielle now, you should get in the habit of calling her that."

"That's gonna be a hard habit to get into, he still looks like a guy, I mean, even with those tits and all..."

"That's not the point, she's our friend, she needs our support."

"You almost called her Ridley yourself, just a second ago."

"Oh shut up, it was a slip." They stop in the middle of the platform and notice that they're the only ones there. Looking at her tired face with make-up smeared and worn away, Benny wants to hurt her somehow. Needs to.

"You think Edgar fucked Dooli tonight," Benny says coldly. "They were in the kitchen a long time with the door closed. And I thought I saw a wet spot on Edgar's pants. What do you think?"

"I think you're being an animal again."

"Comon, I'm curious, I mean it, does Turtle-Head Edgar fuck?...He ever fuck you?"

"What's come over you tonight!? Why are you like this?"

"Like what?"

"Like an asshole."

"Don't call me an asshole."

"Well you're acting like one."

"And I'll pop your face in like one too!"

"Don't threaten me, I'm not coming down to your level."

"And what level's that? What are you, too high and mighty? You think your shit don't stink?"

"Why are you doing this?"

"Doing what? I asked you a simple question, you don't want to answer."

"What question?"

"Did TurtleHead Edgar ever fuck you?"

"And I'm not answering that!"

"Why not?"

"Cause if you don't know the answer then I'm not telling you."

"So then, he did. He probably shoved his thin little dick with a bow tie on the end right up your tight little asshole till you screamed, huh?"

"Fuck you!" She stormed away, stopped at the third pole and looked down the tunnel as the train pulled in. Benny watched her board, then got in the next car and took a seat. He didn't look back cause if she wants to be so fucking high and mighty then let her; maybe some psycho will get on and call her a queer and slice her tender fucking throat open. Thinking this, Benny gets up and goes into her car, but sits away from her. Marybeth throws him a glance and looks down at her folded arms. Across from her sit two grimy transit guys probably right out of the tunnel. Benny noticed them snickering and making cute remarks under their breath as Marybeth sat there pretending she wasn't aware.

Benny didn't move for a couple of minutes till he couldn't take it anymore. He went to sit next to her and he didn't give a shit if the transit guys thought he was queer. He put his hand on her knee and gave it a gentle squeeze. Two stops later the transit guys got up to leave but before they did they both sneaked glances back at the freaks in their midst. Benny touched Marybeth's leg through the run in her stocking. The train stopped and the transit guys got off and once the doors closed behind them they joked to each other. Benny and Marybeth sat there looking down at their feet. As the train slowed for the next stop, they stood at the doors where Benny put his hand on her shoulder and told her she looked tired and she agreed. Near the stairs they came across a woman leaning against the wall, crying up gobs of pain and Benny couldn't imagine what would make somebody so sad. Marybeth squeezed his arm but he told her it was none of their business and it's late and they should just get the fuck home before the morning crowds arrive. Still, Marybeth approached the woman and put her hand on the woman's back. The woman was startled for a moment. Marybeth told her that she didn't want anything from her, didn't want to bother her, that it was alright to cry and to let out the pain, but that she didn't have to cry on a cold stone wall. Then Marybeth put out her arms and the woman collapsed into a sobbing heap. Marybeth held her up and stroked her hair and patted her back and the woman clutched on for life as Benny stood at the pole and watched this perfect stranger sobbing in his wife's arms as if they were sisters. Benny burned up inside, a lump grew in his throat. He thanked the heavens and earth and the moon and the stars and almighty fucking god for putting him in this dirty smelly tunnel with noise and crime and piss and trash and in the middle of it all, Mary-beth, to help him get through. He wondered where the transit guys were now, and the homo-bashers, and the boys from Jersey, and every asshole that ever called her a queer or a fag or a freak or who wanted to cut her up or shoot her dead, cause if they were here maybe they would see that cocks and cunts don't mean a thing. And maybe if the whole fucking world were filled with more freaks like Mary-beth, living wouldn't be so fucked up.

Ridley's mother didn't take too kindly to her son being a woman. She screamed and called him a sicko freak and she blamed his friends and de-manded that his tits be removed. Ridley told her through tears that it's a little late for that. She threatened to cut him off from the money, said he's not part of the family anymore and that he's got no right to call them or contact them—as far as she's concerned her son died in a tragic accident. Ridley screamed that it was an accident of birth and his mother shrieked that she would not accept blame for his sex-perverted illness when her whole life was spent trying to make him normal but he never gave her a chance. If he wants to be a girl so bad he better find a rich husband cause there's nothing worse than a poor pansie in drag. She stormed out of the apartment and down to the street where Wembley, her chauffeur, waited in his gray uniform and bellboy cap and if it wasn't for the wife and kids he's got to feed, he'd tell her to fuck off and die. Instead he opens the door as she glides through life.

The street is heavy tonight. Twice already the cops told them to keep the traffic moving. Benny chugged a beer against the wall and watched the show cause Marybeth was hot in her tight red mini and black high heels. Violet stands off to the side and feels the chill cause she knows she shouldn't even be out here, but as long as she's using rubbers, nobody tells her to leave. Lenny from Seaside wears his bruises and lumps from that attack at Gracie's place. Passing the girls he tells them that Charlie's gonna be alright and that the cops caught the guys who were taken in laughing and joking and showing off their new Ghostbuster haircuts on the news. He says they won't be laughing too hard when they get to Rikers cause then they're gonna know what it is to be attacked. Benny fires his bazooka in the alley and steps out to the street, stares at a wrinkled rubber lying in the gutter with a ring of red lipstick wrapped around it. He kicks it with his foot and Marybeth pulls him away and guides him home.

Ridley was pissed at Marybeth and Benny. He said they're only fair weather friends and now that he's broke they want nothing to do with him. Marybeth tells him he's full of shit and that the only reason they haven't been around is cause they've been working. Benny tells him about the times they've both gone over in the rain and Ridley looks at Marybeth and starts laughing, but Benny doesn't know why. Later they fried their brains and it was the first time Benny could ever remember Ridley not having more drugs than them. In fact, he had none. Ridley was saying how he didn't know what he was gonna do and how his life is ruined and not worth living and when Marybeth told him to get a grip, Ridley snapped that it was a pretty fucking mean thing for her to say. Marybeth told him welcome to reality, this is how most people have to live and it's not worth killing yourself over. But Ridley cried and blubbered how he can't afford to see his shrink and he can't get his change without a doctor's okay and besides he could never afford the operation now anyway. Marybeth sat down next to him and told him to try and relax. Ridley started moaning about time and space and dimensions and he said there was no god and if there was he had a poor sense of humor cause what kind of joke is it to make women men. They played chess but the game was interrupted every half hour when Ridley would lapse into a crying fit and Marybeth would have to hold him and tell him it's gonna be alright.

A few nights later Ridley was dressed in jeans and a baggy shirt—he hadn't shaved and when Marybeth asked him if anything was wrong he told them his mother came by and they had a nice long chat and had reached an understanding: if he agrees to see a new shrink (the one his mother sees) and if he stops altering his body and quits dressing up like a fag—if he tries to be normal—then everything will go back to the way it was with him being rich again. Marybeth said what about your breasts and Ridley said he's having them removed and that he can't afford to be a woman anymore. He also told them he couldn't see them anymore cause the first step to curing himself is to forget the past and start everything fresh. Marybeth argued now who's being the fair weather friend and Ridley snapped back that they were really never his friends cause they were only after his money. Marybeth called him the

worst sort of queen cause he can't even face what he
really is inside. When Ridley asked them to leave
Marybeth wasn't sure if she was more sad or more
furious. Benny held her hand outside and told her
good riddance cause Ridley was a faggot anyway
but Marybeth said that she could understand him
wanting to be rich but not why he'd say those hateful
things about her. Shortly after, Marybeth started
doing Edgar again cause after the party she stopped
doing him but never told him why.

Benny didn't like the color of it as it was cooking. He told her to ditch it but she told him there was
nothing wrong with it. He told her to look at the
black specks, who knows what the fuck it's been
cut with. Marybeth tells him it's good and she's
doing it. He suggests that maybe she should try to
cut back a little and do other things cause everytime he jabs her it feels like Russian roulette, and
one of these days her bullet's gonna come up. Marybeth tells him not to be so dramatic but Benny tells
her it'll be real fucking dramatic at her funeral.
She's running out of spots to jab and all her toes are
getting used up and unless her arms start healing
soon he's gonna have to start jabbing under her
tongue. He fixed her at the table and put the needle
down, touched her cheek and kissed her lips and
she wrapped her arms around him and squeezed

him tight and their tongues locked and he could taste the sweet mint-sugar from the ice cream she ate for lunch. She collapsed in his arms like a dead eel and he carried her off to bed.

Marybeth stumbled awake at the knock on the door. The two young cops standing there sent a shiver down her legs. She caught her voice and asked, "Is anything wrong, officer?"

With a smirk in his eye he asked if Benny Alverez lived there. Marybeth went blank for a moment. He said they were looking for a family member and when Marybeth told them she was his wife they both looked at each other. The first officer said that Benny had been shot breaking into an apartment and was at the hospital and before he could say anything else Marybeth was pushing through the door demanding what hospital and the cops said they'd drive her there. In the car they told her that Benny was shot on his way through the window by the owner's brother-in-law, Frank the ex-cop, who was watching the apartment. Marybeth asked what happened to JR and the one in the passenger seat wrote something down on his pad. Marybeth asked what about the ex-cop with the gun and they told her he'd been arrested for possession cause they found an ounce of coke under the couch and Marybeth asked what about for shooting her husband and neither one of them said anything.

Benny was cuffed to the rail of the bed and Marybeth screamed that her husband was the victim of a crime and they're treating him like an animal but the cops told her Benny was being charged with breaking and entering and that the rules were to cuff him. Marybeth shot back that he was in a fucking coma and if he was somebody important or even if he was Frank the ex-cop he wouldn't have been cuffed, but the cops just shrugged and walked away. Benny was hooked up to all kinds of shit, tubes and meters and bottles hanging over his bed. Marybeth sat at his side and held his hand, repeatedly checking the cuffs, making sure they weren't too tight. She was tempted to lift the bandage on his side and see the wound for herself, but instead she just sat there and quietly sobbed. The doctors didn't know when he'd come out of it or how bad he would be if he did. The only thing left to do was wait and see. Marybeth called Ridley cause she didn't know who else to call or who else would care but when Ridley got on the phone he told her he couldn't talk to her cause how could he be cured if he's constantly hounded by the past. Marybeth slammed down the phone. She tried to call Benny's brother in Washington but his line was disconnected with no forwarding number. She didn't know what to do or where to turn and as her brain started screaming and her body shaking she tried to think of somebody who could bring her a fix, but there was nobody to trust. A nurse came by carrying a tray of pills and Marybeth couldn't wait any longer. She fixed at home on half a dose then went back to the hospital. On the elevator a man and his wife were looking at her through the mirror up in the corner, and seeing her reflection with her eyes dripping black, she couldn't blame them.

Benny just lay there like a statue with the blanket up to his chin. She couldn't even see him breathe. Marybeth cursed him for doing this job without telling her about it and where the fuck was JR cause he seems to have just disappeared. After four days with no change in Benny's condition, a doctor finally ordered the cuffs off telling the cops there's no way this guy is leaving. Twice the nurses tried to make her leave saying she wasn't a family member but Marybeth made such a scene that they let her stay. The only time she did leave was to work or cop her shit. Then it was right back to the hospital where she fixed in the bathroom and sat by his side. He got thinner every day. His face was drawn and yellow, there were bruises on his arm from the tubes and needles. And the smell and the sounds were enough to make her puke. She was sick of hospitals and it seemed like every month she was here visiting one of her friends but nobody ever came to visit Benny. Marybeth felt alone and helpless and she remembered this was how she used to feel before they met, and if she loses him now what's she gonna do, and what kind of world is this where everything is so fucked up and the few times you're happy are small compared to the times you're not. Maybe Ridley was right, she thought. Maybe there is no god cause if there is what's he doing as he watches all this shit happening down here and what does he think as he sees his children shriveling away to skin and bones till their lungs are too weak to fill with air. But then Ridley's an asshole, so she started praying with all her heart, begging him to exist. To hear her and help her and look down on them with sadness and pity cause they needed him now, needed him bad. As she prayed out loud a nurse came in to check on the bottles and seeing Marybeth clutching the rosary in her fingertips and hearing her cold wet cough, she wondered if Marybeth knew that Benny had tested positive.

IN MYSTERIOUS WAYS

Georgie read the papers today, read about his long lost pal, Sal. Maybe there is a god, he thought, maybe he does exist after all. Cause Sal had had it coming, of that there was no doubt. It was just a matter of time cause they find you no matter where you hide. Georgie limped to the window, his left leg dead as wood, and on certain days he still gets dizzy and pisses his pants for no reason and his dick hangs limp like fucking wet spaghetti and it's all because of his long lost friend. You wouldn't recognize him, not the Sal that Georgie knew anyway. From the picture in the paper Sal had grown a beard and gained forty pounds. He died with his eyes wide open which only made him uglier. And as Georgie looked away from the paper to the street, at the girls and the whores and the kids down below, he thought, yup, maybe there is a god, maybe he does exist after all.

Sal had been a small time hood running weed and blow, but when you work for them they don't like you using so Sal was courting danger from the beginning. He was locked in pretty tight from porking Lou the Greek's daughter and when Sal said he would marry her she was happy and for that Louie let him live. But Sal had ambitions, moving grams was not his bag, so he set up his own deals and dropped big names and nobody would fuck with him as long as he was locked in. This was all after the "Georgie Incident" which was old news and forgotten by now. Forgotten by all except Georgie cause he lives it everyday and when he sees people walking and running and doing things he used to be able to do, he wants to get Sal's body and cut off his balls and stuff them in his mouth like Sal once did to that queer in the municipal parking lot off of Stuyvesant.

Georgie and Sal were partners once, dealing weed in Staten Island, the forgotten borough. Georgie and Sal, they had it all. That is, until Sal got greedy and didn't want a partner cause he said that he was doing all the blood work and when somebody needed to be leaned on it was Sal who did the leaning. And Sal resented when Georgie would tell him to cool it with the shit cause Sal was smoking and snorting and shooting the profits and giving it away to chicks he wanted to fuck. The tension mounted, heads were butting and Sal was getting more fucked up and wild and then paranoid so that he didn't trust anybody. He thought they were all out to get him, especially Georgie. So Sal devised a plan.

One night he went to Georgie's home when Georgie was in Jersey. Sal raped his wife in every room and took pictures of her sucking his dick. When Georgie came home she was hysterical, crying and screaming about what happened, and when Georgie went hunting after him, Sal shot him in the back in self-defense—cause that was Sal's specialty. The cops came in and closed their shop and that's when The Boys with the bent noses got involved. They had a meeting where they told Sal and Georgie to cool it or else they'd be fighting it out in Hell. Georgie screamed about being shot in the back and his wife being raped but Sal said that she was the one who came on to him—he was only doing what she wanted him to. The Boys said they didn't want to know about any of this shit, they just wanted the money flowing in. They told Georgie to take a vacation and let Sal run things for a while cause he was locked in with Lou the Greek's daughter, and nobody wanted to fuck with Lou the Greek.

Two years later Georgie's wife left him cause every few months a picture would turn up and she would scream that she couldn't take living with a sexless gimp who'd let her get raped by a two-bit punk and do nothing about it. So now he lives alone in his dungeon hole apartment where he limps up and down the stairs to get in and out and it takes him fifteen minutes each way.

Georgie closed the paper and looked out the window and had tears in his eyes he was so happy. He cut out the picture and taped it on the wall. He would stare at it for hours, study the holes in Sal's body and imagine he was there as it was happening. He'd imagine that he was pulling the trigger and with each jolt of lead, he'd see the blood and the terror and the moment of death in Sal's face. He'd watch the life drip from his eyes as they turn glassy and still, wide open like an idiot's, and smell the burning powder as it floats away taking Sal with it. God, if Georgie could cum he'd be squirting the walls by now. He opened the paper and read the story again, slowly, without the speeding excitement of the first time when his fingers were shaking and his bowels let go from the thrill.

Sal had been trying to move up to keys but nobody would trust him with quantity, he was too crazy. So he figured he would do it on his own and fuck everybody else. That was his first mistake. He was meeting this guy to set up a buy but the guy was complaining that the sample was shit and he wasn't gonna pay for two keys of shit. Well, Sal didn't like this, not one bit, something was wrong and his instincts told him to act. He hatched a plan and played it cool and promised a purer cut on the next night. He met the guy on a cold lonely road, got into his car and sat there for a minute before calling him a fucking deadass nigger snitch for trying to set him up. He pumped two bullets into the back of his head and left him slumped over the wheel with the blood pouring down his shirt. Sal hopped out and took off in his car and went to a late night diner for some eggs. Fucking Sal, he thought The Boys would be happy and shaking his hand. But Sal was in for an awakening.

Sal got no thank you. He fucked with the wrong guy.

An agent from the D-E-A was shot down like an R-A-T and now Sal had to dis-a-ppear. And real quick. The newspapers plastered this one all over and there was nowhere for Sal to hide cause this DEA agent had a wife and kids and everyfuckingbody was out looking for Sal. When he saw himself on tv he was glad they were using the picture from the gym where he's all pumped up and you could see his cut pecs. He hid in a basement cellar till he grew his beard and changed his looks and everybody thought he was in Puerto Rico which he couldn't understand since they know he hates Puerto Ricans. He spoke to his wife over the phone and explained that he was cool, that he had to kill the guy in self-defense and that he couldn't see her or their baby yet cause The Feds would be all over her ass waiting for it. She tried to tell him that if he's innocent then a good lawyer can get him off but it wasn't the law that Sal was worried about.

The papers screamed about the funeral march and had pictures of his kids as they cried on his coffin and all the suits came out of their mansions to make winded speeches that nobody heard. Sal was in the big time now. The heat was so intense nobody could take a piss without starting a fire. When they took in Lou the Greek's daughter and kept her for hours threatening to lock her up even though she hadn't seen Sal in over a year, Lou the Greek got really pissed cause he didn't want his little baby caught up in this shit. That's when The Boys wanted to know how the fuck Lou the Greek could be involved. Sal was making them all look bad. The blonde on tv kept the story alive and reported her updates as if they were news so the cops and The Boys were repeatedly blasted with pictures and rumors and sightings and weirdos and people were calling in with visions of Sal in their dreams. Things were getting out of hand: the gambling and sharking and whoring and dealing trickled down to nothing and soon the whole gang was up in arms and pissed as shit and though they couldn't find

Sal, they all knew where Lou the Greek lived. And Lou was getting nervous. This thing wasn't going away, people weren't forgetting. Sal's wife got on the news and pleaded for understanding, saying how her husband was set up by the cops and that it was all some kind of plot to kill one of their own then go after Sal for it. Things were getting weirder by the minute. Everyday there was a new arrest or another sighting and everything was getting hotter and hotter. The busts were taking place every hour and the cops didn't care if you had a kilo or a seed, they were taking you in. Lou the Greek started losing tribute: the money was late or in the mail, or it just wasn't coming, and Lou knew they were setting him up for the fall so he started making friends. And there were plenty of young turks only too happy to impress Lou the Greek and help him out of this jam. Soon there were Wop-hoods everywhere and you never saw so many armed Italians in one place before. They were spreading out and digging in and leaning on the small-time boys, telling them if they know something they better spill it cause if they're holding info then they're as dead as Sal is gonna be. The Feds started threatening that if The Boys take out Sal there's gonna be even more trouble cause they got this new law they wanna try out: if you kill a cop then you fry like a fish. And they had a chair with Sal's name on it. But The Boys didn't want to see that happen, cause then Sal would get a lawyer and a stay and an appeal and then another and he'd be tying this thing up with writs and corpuses and who-the-fuck knows what for years. They couldn't have Sal talking and trying to make deals cause if Lou or any of his friends were named then things were gonna get even hotter. It became a fucking contest between The Boys and The Feds and Georgie watched it all with trembling limbs cause either way he wins. Sal became a national star when they created a tv show about him and gave out numbers to call if Sal should show his face. He was more famous than the boys from Queens. For months there were twisted arms and broken bones and busted faces but nobody knew where he was. Some thought he was in Florida, or that he'd left the country, but fucking Sal was right under their noses only forty blocks away living like a king in a nice size apartment eating and sleeping and watching movies and sneaking off at night to exchange notes with his mother. Shit, when Georgie read how close he'd been—he knew the building—he wanted to scream cause he could've limped down there and caught Sal coming out at night and he could've shot his dick off and watched him bleed in the street instead of in the papers. That's how they got him, sneaking off at night for a meeting with mom and destiny. He got it cold, he got it fast, he got it good.

Georgie closed the paper and took a deep breath. It was all too good, too rich, and he couldn't remember the last time he'd felt so whole. He was tempted to call up his wife and tell her that he still loved her and how sorry he was and maybe she would be glad to hear from him and forget about everything else and come back, but he didn't know where she was or how to reach her. Then he felt it on his ankle, like a warm liquid sock. He shook his leg and kicked off his shoe. Those goddamn fucking piss bags. He cleaned himself and changed his bag and went out to pick up his medicine, legal stuff, from his doctor. He ambled along, with his cane on the curb, past the stores and the garbage. He stopped at the newsstand and bought two more papers. Turning the corner the kids started doing his walk and calling him The Piss Man. But Georgie was too happy to let anything ruin it. He came out of the drugstore, popped two in the alley, went over to the liquor store and bought a fifth of Red. On the way home he saw Tony the Wop strutting like a peacock spewing how his friends took care of Sal and how he was in on it and knew all about it before it happened, and just as Tony lets fly with a piece of minestrone noodle, Georgie tells him not now I gotta go. Home. To start the festivities, the celebration, the first night of Sal's violent death. He turned on the news and slugged from his bottle and popped two more pills and rolled up a joint till he couldn't stand up. He reread the papers and stared at the pictures and finished his bottle then stubbed out the roach. Liquor passes right through him, it has a direct line right out of his system. He could see the bag bulging under his pants leg filled and ready to break. He hobbled over and banged into the table. The bag broke off from the tube and spilled on the floor and Georgie collapsed in the puddle. But he wasn't mad, in fact he was the opposite: warmed with the Spirit and cheeks all red rosy and eyes filled with water and laughing and joking and heaving and choking in his own piss just thinking about it, the absolute perfection of it. The Holy Symmetry of it. And staring up at the news picture, a light clicked inside and it opened his heart where his soul couldn't hide. In the blink of an eye that it took Sal to fire, to leave a wife and her children no husband and father, for their home to be empty and quiet with crying...in that second when Sal felt the bullets rip through, with his eyes glazed in terror, his skin turning blue—leaving a wife and child of his own—in the flash that it took for these things to happen, Georgie found his god. Then he laughed out a prayer and he clutched at his hair and he watched as his piss oozed out into the hall.

THE PSALM OF
RICHARD THE EXECUTIVE

Richard the Executive, he's pretty fucking sick. He cruises down on West Street and makes children suck his dick.

Then he goes back to his wife and kid in his nice Long Island home, pretending to be normal. Acting the part. With all his heart. Cause Richard the Executive is pretty fucking sick.

He's into piss, he's into shit, he's into pins right through his tit. He likes pain as much as the next guy. Don't ask why.

He likes them young and thin and weak cause they do more. And they need more, and drugs are money, and money talks and nobody walks and Richard stalks with his evil blackened soul sticking out of his pants like a fucking big dick cock of death shooting acid-cum from hell. But Richard belongs to the Lodge. His son is a boyscout. And his wife never took it up the ass cause she's much too respectable for that.

Richard drives a red sedan, he thinks it makes him younger. He parks right near the water and then waits for younger brothers. Once inside he takes them to his place deep in the city. They strip and whip and fuck and suck and Richard dresses up like a woman and makes them fuck him again. Cause Richard's working late tonight, and drugs are money.

There's Danny Boy his favorite toy cause Danny's into crying. For seven blasts he'll suck you fast and Richard sends him flying. Then Richard takes it up the ass and though he's using condoms, for thirteen months he didn't so who knows what the fuck he's got or giving. He doesn't care cause that fucking urge is too strong to resist. And the danger makes it stranger. And better. And wetter. Richard buys Danny some clothes and lets him take a shower, then he lays in the tub and tells Danny to piss on him as he pretends it's Niagara Falls and he's a newlywed.

Richard shaves his pubic hairs and paints his face and paints his nails and wears a purple afro wig and lets himself be dogged by Tito Mendez with the thirteen inch cock, and for an extra hundred Tito cums on his face while Richard cries and licks at his tears. It's that demon inside that makes him hide and rips his pride and opens wide his reddish eyes. Those eyes that plead the need and feed the greed and plant the seed cause Richard hates himself and hurts himself and punishment is pleasure. And one of these days he's gonna hate himself so fucking much that he's gonna kill somefuckingbody and dump their rotting-feces-oozing-corpse in the goddamn sewer. Then Richard will be cured.

Maybe.

CHUCKIE'S IN LOVE AND RUINS

Chuckie broke his eyeglasses last night, in that fight with who-the-fuck-knows. The guy came up and wanted money and Chuckie had none to spare and lucky for him the blade broke off at the first lunge cause as they went at it hand to hand the guy realized it wasn't worth it and ran away. Chuckie taped his glasses with a dirty band-aid and now he wears them crooked, but the world seems straighter to him this way. He ties his boots with wire cause the laces broke two months ago. He roams the Broadway strip in search of meaning, cause Chuckie's got no life. He walks for hours that become days and the only time he stops is when he's sleeping or copping or smoking his hits and everything he owns is on his back cause Chuckie's a one-man-world.

And nothing ever bothers him cause he takes it all in stride.

Chuckie gets his money from bottles, cans, and begging. He does alright at begging cause he doesn't look like a washed-up bum. He's neat and polite and people don't mind giving him some loose change which he gladly takes to cop his smoke and buy his fifth and to keep on walking till it gets too late or he's too fucked up. Chuckie sleeps off West Street in this big dark place only the homeless know about. It's dirty and smelly and nobody who's got someplace better would even want to see it in their nightmares, but it's home to Chuckie.

Every few weeks he goes to see his ex-wife and she always tries to give him money but he refuses unless he's really broke. See, she still loves him, just not as a husband. But Chuckie loves her with all his heart and soul and mind and guts and all-that-she-is-and-will-be is what consumes his every thought and it's that loss that screams out and rips its teeth into his stomach till there's a giant bleeding hole that the wind sweeps through.

All the whores like Chuckie cause he'll turn them on for free. He's nice to queers, polite to trans, a regular likable guy. He just doesn't have a life. He used to though, when he and Jane were together, up through school as real close friends. In the beginning they would tell each other of the different people they were fucking and whether they were good or not, and quite by accident their friendship got sweaty. They fell in love holding hands with star crossed eyes, and it was heaven. Till they got married. Cause things don't go like they're supposed to. Chuckie was getting his degree in business soon and thought he'd be sure to make great money, but after four years of waiting for his ship-to-come-in and money-around-the-corner, Jane got tired cause all she knew was that she was working ten hours a day at Macy's, and she was the one making more. When that option deal collapsed and all the bosses got off free, Chuckie took the fall. He didn't go to jail but he had to leave the firm, which put him back to square one. So he spent his time working even harder till he and Jane drifted so far apart they were strangers. It broke his heart and mind to go, but he left without a fight cause it was only a trial she told him. Chuckie thought he'd be back in weeks. That was almost a year ago. Once his money ran out he left the hotel and hung out for three days on the street cause without her nothing else mattered. He tried the shelters and kitchens and was robbed and cut and realized he was safer outside.

Chuckie stepped into the deli and Remo was already cursing and saying for crying out loud these fucking bums with their cans are driving me crazy and why don't they go the fuck to the chinks across the street. Chuckie smiled and handed him the bag as he grunted and grumbled then gave Chuckie fifty cents. Chuckie bought a Hershey bar for lunch.

He begs on Fifth in the forties and people give him coins. He walks down to the station underground and while he's in the neighborhood he figures he might as well stop in and see Jane. Lingerie section, row seventeen. The coins in his pocket jingle like bells as he skirts through the aisles and people wonder where the sound is coming from. Passing the dummies all pretty and hard with their faces in passion and clothes on display, he wishes he had launched a rocket cause in another second he's gonna wish he were dead. He stops at the counter and glances around and after a second she steps into view. He catches her long wavy hair like a curtain of silk and her milky complexion, simple and pure, just a touch of eye liner and a smidgeon of blush; she didn't see him at first cause she was talking to a lady so he stood at the counter and watched from afar. The hole in his stomach was growing like acid, his guts and his heart melting away and he could feel that icy cold wind sweeping through and taking his soul out the door. But the smile remained on his face, a dummy on display, and when she turned and saw him she let out a crooked little smile and the universe stopped for a moment...

Till Chuckie cut a path through the tension.

She took him aside for a short little chat and asked how he's doing and told him he's looking good and does he need anything and how is he set for money. Chuckie swallowed the lump in his throat and told her he was fine and that she's more beautiful than ever. She asked him where he was living and what would he be doing for the winter and how long is he gonna be punishing himself cause in some ways she still blames herself for what happened. Chuckie didn't answer, but asked her out to lunch. She said the store's been real busy and she can't get away. Chuckie told her to make sure she's eating right cause she looks a little thin but she told him not to worry about her cause he's the one with problems. When she opened her purse he closed it in her hands. A woman was calling from a rack of things she had no right to wear, and as Jane looked over Chuckie knew it was time to go. He said goodbye and told her not to worry cause he's doing fine, and he walked away as Jane went to her customer. Halfway through the store he stopped and turned around. He watched her take out lacy black things of velvet and silk and feel them against her face and her cheek and her lips and her teeth and her breasts and her waist and her thighs and Chuckie wanted to be with her and have children with her and live forever with her and everything that could have been squeezed his guts till he was suffocating. Then when the muzak speakers spit out Sinatra singing Cycles and every fucking word seemed to fit Chuckie to a tee, he thought about when their lives were one and everything they did and planned was together and everything he knew she knew cause they were part of each other in every way with their families and friends and their future. God, at one time she loved him so fucking much, so fucking much indeed. In those days she couldn't pass him without touching him or kissing him or rubbing his shoulders. She was always there supporting him and loving him and fooling and joking and laughing and they were happy, so truly happy. He drove himself crazy trying to figure out how he fucked it up. He was good to her; he never hit her or cheated or clung too hard and how can love just die like a flower that wilts and shrivels in the fucking dirt. Watching her face he could smell her perfume and her strawberry hair, see the gleam in her eye that used to be his and his alone, and in his mind he was back with her in the apartment, and she was asking him to close the cabinets he took pride in leaving open, or to take out the garbage he'd forgotten, or any other stupid chore that if asked today he'd give his right arm to

do. All the times when he hurt her or said something cruel, all the times when he could have done
something nice but didn't, everything he should
have said when it mattered, when he had the chance,
if only if only if only...These were the nightmares
that pecked at his brain and as long as he's moving
he won't go insane so he roams down the street with
a hole in his guts and a cup in his hand for the
smoke in his lungs.

He grubbed his way back up and copped four
blasts from sexy Eileen McDermott who wanted
him bad. But Eileen's husband ran a murder crew
and nobody in their right or sick mind would fuck
with Eileen. Then Chuckie went East.

He made a pipe from foil and straws and crouched
down behind the trash bags at the Korean pizza
place. He fried his brain on two blasts worth and
ditched his pipe and sat in the garbage till he had to
pee. Chuckie was flying so high he pissed off the
earth and it trickled into the darkness and vacuum
of star studded space till it found a new home on
some concrete planet where it crushed and destroyed every living thing. Chuckie watched in the
window as Suck My Wang twirled the dough with
his white powdered fingers, making it grow just
like the Wops. He greased it and sauced it and covered it with the most disgusting of toppings like
spinach and broccoli and weird green things that

Chuckie couldn't even figure out what the fuck they were. For a second he was tempted to barge in and ask them what the hell are they doing to pizza, but is startled by Wendy Washington, who's standing next to him. She doesn't look so good tonight, though she gives him a smile and says hello.

He made a new pipe in the back of the hall and the matches he lit were the only light. Wendy, black as night, couldn't be seen but felt, cause she was all touchy and feely and rubbing him and breathing close and wanting him to fuck her cause it's been three weeks since she's been fucked by a man who didn't hate her guts. Chuckie turned her on to his last two blasts and they sat in silence creating pictures in their minds of when they were happy—or at least in different places. She melted on top of him and found his neck with her tongue and licked his lips and in the dark Chuckie thought she was Jane. She moved down to his pants and he put out his legs and within seconds he was in her mouth and out of his mind cause Jane would never do it like that; Jane was gentle, and soft, but Wendy's sucking like she wants to rip her lungs apart. He cries limp as shit and Wendy wants to know what the problem is but he won't tell her. She slides across the hall and scratches her pussy as Chuckie zips his fly. They sit there for an hour till Wendy gets straight and softly gets up and leaves for the street.

Chuckie wakes to a dog sniffing his leg and in the dark he's afraid to move so he lies there trembling like an epileptic. The dog starts growling and Chuckie wishes he had a knife. The dog pokes his nose and growls louder then leans back to pounce and just as Chuckie tries to slide away it attacks and rips at his feet. Chuckie kicks and punches and he can feel the teeth shredding his pants and breaking his skin and he jumps up beating the dog off his arm as he runs to the door. A voice calls out for King to heel and Chuckie looks back to see someone standing at the top of the stairs watching the whole time. King stands there with his bloody teeth in view. Chuckie yells up why the fuck d'you let your dog attack me for Chrissakes and the guy says that he doesn't want any drug addict bums sleeping in his hallway and if Chuckie ever comes back he'll get King after him again but he won't tell him to heel next time. Chuckie steps out and feels the blood freezing to his legs. He checks the rips in his pants and notices that his front pocket has been sliced open and all his money's gone. He felt like crying but it was too cold, so he kept moving instead.

The rumble in his stomach pulled him into the hot bagel place and standing there warming up he asks for a scrap of bagel and promises to pay for it later, but they tell him to get the fuck out cause he's getting blood on the floor. He takes some napkins from the counter and leaves. Sitting on the stoop he wipes his legs and in the cold they don't hurt as much but once the sun comes out things'll heat up. He watches daybreak over the buildings and wonders what Jane is doing right now. Is she still in bed or just getting up for work; is she lying alone or with her boyfriend, or is she even thinking about him cause maybe she doesn't think about it anymore. From the next block he hears some yelling but it doesn't sound like a fight just like somebody calling for something. A woman comes by walking her puppy on a leash and seeing Chuckie sitting on the stoop all haggard and ripped she crosses with a fearful indifference. Chuckie holds his sliced pocket closed cause the wind is cutting through and freezing his balls. He gets up and starts his walking cause now he's gotta grub an extra few bucks for some pants. He hops the turnstile and eats a crusty donut from the ground then takes the train down to the deuce. It's barely morning but the strip's alive with everybody hawking and selling and begging and threatening and everytime a cop walks by they chill for a moment. Down at Ninth you got Ritters Rejects washing windows while at the tunnel the leather skinned pretzel geeks fight with their carts. The movies don't open till eleven but Show World's open with Vaginal Vivian and her gaping hole that swallows raw eggs. Chuckie stepped in but was thrown out when he didn't buy any tokens. He went next door to warm up and grub the buses but they don't come till later so he hung out with Rico Montoya who's selling his lips for a nickel. Rico lives in the warehouse off West Street and Chuckie once helped him fight off two guys who wanted to slice his ass open with a razor. Rico was only thirteen and nobody knew where he came from or if he had any family. He bought Chuckie a chocolate shake then asked where he'd been last night and what the fuck happened to his pants and Chuckie told him about the hallway and the dog and Rico spit out a laugh and wanted to go and kill it. A bus pulled in and people were passing and Chuckie went grubbing for some change to go home. Rico stood off with a satisfied smile cause he makes more in an hour than Chuckie does in a day, but then Chuckie doesn't have to take cum in his mouth. As Chuckie went back to the benches to wait for the next bus, he saw Rico walking to the garage with a middle-aged man. By noon Rico was rich and Chuckie had enough for some pants so he went down to Fourth Street and bought a pair used. Soup is free on East Fourth and though it tastes like water Chuckie pretends it's French onion and he's back in France. He searches for cans, and at every red light he asks for some change.

Eileen's waiting with her tiny pert smile and Chuckie cops three blasts to get him to the night. After turning him on she touches his cheek and with sex-in-her-eyes asks where he's been staying and why doesn't he do something else this way he makes free shit and has money for a room.

At sundown the sewers overflow on West Street and Chuckie hangs out watching the girls ply their trade. The wind is blowing and the traffic's rumbling and the girls are shaking in their tiny gold panties with their legs growing goosebumps and their nipples hard as ice. One blonde catches his eye. She's a young new thing he's never seen before and her legs are so fine with a perfect round ass and the cars are stopping and the guy behind is yelling out his window that he saw her first and you better get the fuck away. Chuckie watches with a smile cause it's a fucking jungle out here. He fires a blast and starts leaving his body; floating through darkness he sees visions of colors and if at anytime a vision of Jane would appear he would quickly think of colors again. The cars and the whores and the cops and the johns were doing a ballet of reality which took him out even farther. When he felt the cement under his feet he got up and walked to the warehouse. Passing Munson's diner with the black plate stove and the greasy red burgers, he remembered he was starving which meant he must of been straight which meant it was time to blast another. He climbed through the wall and inside he could see all the fires cause everybody had their own fire. He climbed up a mountain of salt and sat next to Rico's fire. Rico's sitting with a ripped oily tarp draped around him like a blanket and though he's close to the fire, he's still shivering. He has two black eyes and it looks like he's been crying. Chuckie says nothing, he just sits there and pulls out his blast and lights it, passing it to Rico. Two fires away they hear a fight break out and the whole warehouse is screaming and yelling and voices bounce off the rafters like weapons and Rico and Chuckie are the only people not going nuts. They get wasted out of their faces and Rico sucks in that smoke like it's oxygen and he's lost in space. They sit there and stare at the fire which is getting lower by the minute. Chuckie found himself slipping into a Jane vision but caught it in time. He followed a burning ash through the flames and into the night. Rico told him how he was ripped off and beaten by some guy he goes with uptown, a regular that never gave him any trouble before but today goes nuts and pounds his face till he's unconscious. Chuckie doesn't know what to say, so he sits there with no expression. Rico holds himself tight cause he's on the verge of breaking, and Rico never let anyone see him like this. The wind howls through the roof and the traffic speeds on the highway and a siren wails its way to some emergency. Chuckie found himself staring at Rico, at the bruises on his eyes, the welt on his cheek, thinking, he's too young for this shit, he's just a fucking kid and he's living like some kind of monster of humanity. He lit up his last blast and they both smoked it and between the smoke in his lungs and the heat from the fire Chuckie wanted to give him his jacket. Rico picked at a tattered end of the tarp around his shoulders till he ripped it off and dropped it into the flames. He watched it squirm and burn and Chuckie noticed the hint of a smile on his face. The orange tongues licked at his eyes, painting his face in shadow and despair, and in the quiet murky chill of the night, Rico looked for the first time since he'd met him six months ago, like what he was. A child.

Chuckie wanted to say something—anything—to get him out of here, to tell him why the fuck don't you just go home and get away from this shit, that this can't be any kind of life for a kid to have where you're sucking dicks and getting beat up and not knowing when you'll be stabbed in the heart. But watching through the flames the words never came. Maybe what Rico had left was worse. Cause

Chuckie could never imagine the sight of Rico's father shooting his mother dead with five blasts in the face then turning the gun on his older brother and killing him with the last one through the heart; then reloading the gun while Rico locked himself in the bathroom and tried to squeeze out the tiny square window; then the door being kicked open and this hulking mass of sweat with silver dollar eyes all twitching where the pupils were the size of quarters and Rico screaming and begging Daddy please don't kill me till he collapsed in a heap on the floor, his whole body tense and waiting for deliverance. Then in a deep raspy voice his father crying out, now nobody's gonna have her! then a scream and a gunshot and a plop and after a moment when Rico knew he wasn't dead yet, peeking through his fingers to see his father spraying the floor with red, to see his foot quivering, the left one, shaking like a dildo. When they found Rico covered in blood and hiding in the tub with the curtain closed, no one could figure out how his mother's body wound up in the closet cause Rico wasn't talking—didn't for six months, not a word. His mother's cousin and her husband took him in and though they weren't bad to him, they weren't good. He knew he was fucking things up cause he overheard them one night talking about having a kid of their own and what kind of influence would he be and there wasn't enough room anyway...

Rico's face sagged, his eyes got heavy, and with the bruises around them he looked like a zombie. Chuckie could see him floating back to who-knows-where cause his eyes were now fluttering. They popped wide open and Rico took another stab at staying awake. Chuckie watched the glowing embers, wished he had some scotch. He was straight, and for a moment he actually thought of pulling himself together and trying to get on with his life and forgetting about Jane and the past and what the fuck is he doing living like this. At the end of the warehouse a woman sobs and Chuckie starts crying and his icy tears burn his face and just as Rico turns onto his belly on the cold rock salt, Chuckie realizes how pathetic he is. At least he had a life and had things and was happy and knows what it is to have someone and to be loved. It's his choice to live this way. But Rico probably had nothing or no one and everyfuckingbody he comes in contact with wants to fuck him or rip him off or cut him open with a razor. And thinking this Chuckie wouldn't trade places with Rico for anything, not even if this mountain of salt became a mountain of blast.

Chuckie could no longer feel his toes. They were

numb. He tucked the tarp around Rico's sides and patted his head. Looking across the huge expanse of the warehouse, with the smoldering fires and the dark huddled figures around them, Chuckie went to get some wood.

BULLETS AND BRUTALITY

Romeo had all this heat building inside of him, boiling to the top, and if he didn't release it he was gonna explode into a million tiny fragments. So last night he launched four rockets in a row and went to cardboard town with Brazil. It was just lying there, alone, drunk, and Romeo could see the strings of snot dripping down its cheek. Brazil kicked its feet to wake it but it just mumbled and rolled over. Romeo took a two-by-four and started beating the living shit out of it till its legs and arms were broken and its head was bleeding. Brazil kicked it with all his might in the balls and when it flopped onto its stomach Romeo started pounding the board on its spine trying to snap it. God, it felt so fucking good, so fucking good inside. Before they left, Brazil tried to light it on fire but its shirt wouldn't catch, then he tried to light up its hair but it just singed. Kneeling down near the dripping head Romeo could hear a deep wheezing gurgle from inside its lungs.

Romeo's mother was sitting on the couch with his sister Joy beside her. Romeo said nothing as he stepped in. His mother wouldn't look up, she just stared at the pillow clutched to her gut, cause she wasn't sure if she could ever get over this one, her youngest, her baby. Joy went to the kitchen to make a call and Romeo followed to eat.

Joy dials a number while Romeo picks through the fridge. She turns around and leans against the wall holding the phone to her ear, watching him with poisonous eyes. He can feel them on his shoulder, the heat from the pupils melting into his skull, the hate, like a seed planted in his brain, a memory tattoo. He wanted to pop her so bad in the face, to haul off and give her one lasting shot for history and knock her fucking teeth into the back of her skull cause how the fuck could she blame him for the fucked up shit that happens out there. And shit, it's been over a week, time to forget the past and worry about tomorrow. As Joy puts the phone down and goes back inside, Romeo drinks a glass of chilled water at the table.

Later they all meet at the houses and Soby's there straight from the hospital with his eyes all glassy red and he looks like death come to life. Brazil rolls a joint and spreads some hash oil on top, lights it, and they all toke except for Cremont who says he only tokes rockets into his lungs. They goof on him for being a snob-ass pussy but Cremont says fuck you and pulls out a fistful of rockets and starts lighting them up and then they all pull out their rockets and blow the houses to kingdom come. Romeo tells them they need to do a job tonight and no one disagrees.

With his brains on alert and his nerves feeling fuzzy, Romeo waits near the corner with three in the alley and everytime a stranger passes he sizes them up. Romeo shoves the third one against the wall and holds a gun in his terrified face and before he can breathe the others are emptying his pockets and Romeo keeps his eyes locked tight cause if they ever see this guy again he's dead. Brazil stands there shaking in his pants which is never a good sign. Cremont squeezed the guy's tie till he choked and for a second Brazil thought of taking out his knife and using it. Romeo cocked the gun and the guy started crying and begging for his life and praying to God and Jesus. Romeo ripped him from the wall and sent him off down the street, the guy took off like a bat out of purgatory. They all laughed and counted the money which was thirty-six bucks or nine bucks each. Soby said he wanted to get laid cause in the hospital the only thing he could get was blow jobs, and no one disagreed.

They swept through the street and everybody stepped aside cause sweeping they look like the end of the world. Seeing a pack of hungry dogs picking through the garbage and fighting over the scraps Brazil wondered if they'd eat a human hand if he got them one. Soby grabbed Debbie Carter from the playground and pulled her by the arm through the hole in the fence and once she saw the others standing there she stopped and said she wasn't doing everybody, she was just doing Soby. Soby pushed her to the dirt and pulled her clothes off and when she tried to sit up he slapped her and threw her down again. He ripped her blouse and she was yelling at him not to rip her clothes cause she would take them off by herself. Brazil was telling her to shut up bitch, and he had that look in his eye, so Debbie shut her mouth. Soby stood over her and let her undo her bra, then she undid her pants and with much effort shimmied them down to her ankles. Romeo and Brazil teased and howled for her to take it all off, which after Soby threatened to pop her face, she did. She sat there naked while they stood around admiring and taunting and for a second she thought of trying to escape. Soby knelt down and spread her legs and while the other three launched a rocket, he fucked her. When he was finished, Romeo got on top and Debbie asked for a blast please but Romeo told her to suck his dick if she wants a blast so bad, then he stuck it in her mouth. Brazil was watching and smoking and trembling and you could tell he was fucking wired. Debbie cried as Romeo raped her and nobody told her to stop cause they were enjoying it. Brazil lifted her to her knees and bent her over then raped her up the ass and by now Debbie was moaning as if she were dying inside. Her face was scraped and her hair was matted and the tears and the dirt were smeared on her cheeks and Brazil pounded his fists on her back with every brutal thrust. While she's being raped from behind, Soby puts the pipe to her lips but she doesn't toke. Brazil slides out and takes her panties from the ground and cleans himself with them. Debbie collapsed to her side and lay there like a rack of lamb and Cremont yells that he always goes last. Romeo tells him to shut up and fuck the bitch, then he lights another. When Cremont was finished he stood back and Debbie rolled onto her belly and cried in her arms. They were about to leave when Brazil took out his dick and pissed all over her back and head. Soby dropped a couple rockets near her face and they left.

Romeo stuck his key in the lock but when he opened the door it was chained. He started banging it and screaming like a maniac. Cremont stood back to kick it in and just as Old Man Rutherford reached it, the door burst open smashing him in the face and knocking him down. They swarmed in and stood around him like vultures. He was groggy and bleeding from the nose, he slowly sat up and spit out a tooth. Romeo pulled him to his feet and threw him onto the couch with such force that his head banged against the wall and everything went black for a second. Brazil took things out of the fridge and threw them on the floor. Romeo and Soby went through his drawers looking for anything they might have missed on Tuesday. Soby ripped out clothes from closets and drawers and threw them across the room. Rutherford sat on the couch and watched Cremont launch a rocket. Brazil took the cough syrup and scarfed it in one shot before smashing the bottle against the wall over Mr. Rutherford's head, who sat there trembling and picking the pieces of glass from his white hair. Romeo sat next to him, put his arm around him like they were long lost friends, then with a dripping cheshire smile, he demands the check. His smile slowly dips as Rutherford stutters that he spent it on rent and food; the others start making warning sounds cause they're not too pleased to hear this either. Brazil takes out his knife and clicks it open and Rutherford's eyes go wide, but Romeo motions him away. In a calm and quiet voice he explains to

Rutherford that those aren't the rules, that the rules are that he's supposed to give them his check and then they'll decide when he pays his rent and buys his food. Before Rutherford can say anything else Romeo rips a clump of hair from his head and smacks his face, and getting snot on his hand he grabs Rutherford by the shirt and flings him across the room where Brazil steps on his neck till he heaves up his dinner of tea and toast. Rutherford lies there crying and begging for God to save him and how could he work his whole damn life at an honest job and pay his taxes and do everyfucking-thing right only to be left at the mercy of these fucking monsters from hell. Soby steps out of the bathroom with a filled enema bag and stands over Rutherford and pulls the old man's pants down. Brazil keeps his foot on Rutherford's neck as Soby forces it in and squeezes the bag as Rutherford bangs the floor with his open palm. Romeo and Cremont sit on the couch watching tv, and Cremont jerks off till he cums on Teri Garr's face. Soby gives the bag one last hard squeeze and Rutherford convulses on the floor, sobbing with everything inside, which ain't much. They finally let him go and he drags himself like a wounded dog into the bathroom where the seat has been missing for weeks. He lifts himself onto the cold porcelain and sitting in the icy water he releases himself. Soby tries to open a window but it's stuck so Brazil takes an empty jar of mustard and chucks it through. Rutherford's weeping in his hands and for a second he considers taking a razor to his throat cause he doesn't know how much more of this he can take. Romeo steps into the bathroom and almost pukes. He warns Rutherford that if there's ever a chain on his door again, or if his check ain't ready and waiting for them, or if he calls the cops or tells any-fuckingbody what they do, he's gonna be strung upside down and stripped naked then cut up with razor blades till he drowns on his own blood dripping into his nose. Brazil chucked the tv out the window where it smashed in the alley. As Romeo closed the door behind him, he could hear Rutherford in the bathroom whimpering like a woman.

Caesar's limo drove past and Cremont called him a queer cause he's always wearing purple. Brazil threw a bottle but it missed and smashed in the street. They hung out till morning just smoking and laughing and hassling anybody that passed. On the way home it occurred to Romeo that it's as if Ledell never even existed.

His mother was sleeping on the couch as he quietly slipped in. Joy was gone and probably sleeping with any bastard who would have her. He went to his room and in the quiet dark of morning, started putting Ledell's things away, folding up his cot, getting rid of any trace except the picture on the mirror where they're both wearing their colors and Romeo's holding a knife to his throat. Fucking Ledell, he should've been more careful, he should've been watching his back. He was only 11 years old. Romeo lay down with his sneakers on the bed, hands behind his head, and tried to sleep. But everytime he closed his eyes, tried to close his mind, he couldn't stop the sounds. The pop, the scream, the yelling, and the images gushing out like blood from a severed vein with the entire block on fire, and Romeo pulling his gun and running like a cat and looking for any fucker running away and seeing that lady screaming with her hand over her mouth and trying not to look at the body but unable to look away, and the tiny hole in the back of the neck cause that's how they do it now, and Romeo kneeling down and seeing the saliva bubbling out of his brother's mouth and the stream pouring out of his neck and holding him tight and trying to smack him awake and the crowd standing around but keeping their distance, and the crew running up and taking positions with their guns out ready to blow away anyfuckingbody who tried to get near, and Romeo feeling the cold dead weight in his hands and letting it sag to the pavement and standing up and wiping the blood on his pants and hearing sirens approach from a few blocks away he grabs the gun on the ground and takes off with the others following.

Romeo lies in sweat, wide awake though his body's exhausted. His heart pounds and the rage inside is burning and he has to do something soon before it swallows him whole. He hears his mother get up and go into the bathroom and after a few seconds of running water she comes out and goes back to the couch. He launches a rocket out the window, and to the melody of his mother's crying, he falls off to sleep.

Sammy wanted to see them the next day and Romeo told them to be on time cause meetings with Sammy were important. Sammy's surrounded by his lieutenants and his zooka boys; Luckyfoot fixes the base and there's all kinds of quantity and automatic guns and piles of cold cash lying around. Sammy's with his mother and when she opens her bag to blow her nose, Romeo sees a shiny gold-handled 9mm semi. Sammy has a job he wants them to do and when Brazil asks why doesn't he get his zooka boys to do it Sammy tells him questions may be hazardous to his health, but he says it with a smile. They all get fucked out of their faces on primo- pure base and Sammy tells Romeo how sorry he is about his brother and that he'll do anything he can to see that the fucker suffers. He tells them how much he appreciates them keeping the neigh-

borhood cool for his zooka boys and making sure
nobody tries to fuck around and he wishes it was
like that all over but it ain't. He tells them about this
guy named Pepperton who's been annoying him.
Pepperton was a guy who'd been copping large
amounts and the last shipment from Sammy was
bad cause the chemists fucked up somewhere and
when Pepperton wanted his money back Sammy
said no way. But Pepperton goes ballistic and starts
popping people like balloons. Sammy stopped talking and the room got real quiet for a moment, till
Romeo told him not to give it another thought.
Sammy smiled and stepped over to his mother who'd
been watching the whole time. She opens her purse
and takes out the gold handled 9, a beautiful piece,
deadly, and Brazil's eyes bugged out of his face as
Sammy gave it to Romeo. Romeo felt it in his hand
and saw it gleam in the light and when he looked
back up at Sammy, he had a tear in his eye. Sammy
choked out a cackle and gave them each a thousand
bucks in cash.

As they cut through the alley Romeo slid out the
clip and let them take turns pulling the trigger.
Brazil wanted a bullet but Romeo told him he wanted
to be the first and Brazil called him a pussy. It was
almost three so they went to the school. Standing
out front is Cokie Cola dealing his beat grams and
nickels to the learning crowd. Soby laughs to him-

self cause Cokie's been out here forever and will probably outlive them all. As they pass, Romeo tells Cokie he's putting on some weight and he don't mean in the drug department. Cokie smiles through his gums and tells them they should finish school and get their diplomas but Brazil tells him to fuck his dead mother's corpse. Romeo slices through the crowd looking from side to side like a shark in the water and if he sees just one face he doesn't like, it's getting popped. The kids are yelling and calling to their friends, some are bouncing balls, and standing in the middle of it all, Romeo feels like an old man. He steps out of the side door to see Mrs. Hennonlot and her sexy calves in those high heel shoes and he wants to rape her just as bad as he did when he was in school—if only it were night and she were alone. Brazil pulled a girl from the crowd and was talking to her near the gate and from the looks of it, it was personal. Romeo gets tapped from behind and for a second he's tempted to whirl a fist but something stops him. When he turns around Becky smiles at him and his eyes tell her how close she came to getting popped.

"You wouldn't hit me, would you?" she asks.

"If I didn't know it was you, fuck yeah."

"Wow, you're tough," she says sarcastically. She gives him a sideways glance and he smiles; Becky was the only one who could do that. They went out the back gate and through the lot. Romeo launched a rocket and they toked. Behind the houses there's a patch of grass near the fuse boxes. Romeo held her tight and looking into her dark doe eyes and her soft puffy cheeks as smooth as creamy chocolate, he knew if there were any one person in the world he didn't want to hurt, it was her. He kissed her and guided her down and looking up at him, she coyly asked what he was gonna do. They fucked and Romeo lay there leaning on his side and everytime she looked at him he couldn't figure out how he could love her so fucking much one minute and hate her the next. He lay on his back with his hands behind his head and stared up at the wires. He couldn't take her eyes anymore. He wanted to fuck her again, only this time hard, and deep; he wanted to hurt her and rip that softness off her face and leave her crying with her pussy sore. Instead he told her to suck his dick but she wouldn't.

"What's the big fuckin' deal, you just fucked the shit outta me, now you don't wanna suck my dick."

"Cause you're being an animal about it!"

"And that's the best time to do it, don't be a fuckin' bitch. Suck my dick!"

"No, fuck you." She sat up and buttoned her blouse and when she noticed Romeo watching her she turned her back.

"You prick tease," he called her. "I could make you suck it."

"Fuck you, I'm not sucking your dick and I wouldn't suck it if it was the last piece of food on earth and I was starving."

She turned around and fastened her pants. Romeo could see that her mind was solid on this, and whether he raped her or killed her she still wouldn't change it. He loved that about her. It turned him on. Watching her turn and walk away without a word, he thought of how much he wanted to fuck her again and how much he loved her and wanted to put a baby in her guts cause then she'd really be his; she'd be tied down to him and he could put her up in a place or maybe just give her Rutherford's place so he can visit her and be her husband when he wants, or just get up and split. He pissed against the fuse boxes then went to the others.

Cremont's brother Tipsy stood in front of the store toking his dirtweed as Romeo stepped up and slapped the back of his head. Tipsy turned around and told Romeo to watch himself before he gets his ass kicked which prompted Romeo to start throwing slaps and soft punches and Tipsy was overwhelmed with fingers in his face till he said he was sorry. He passed the joint to Romeo who spit it out after one toke.

"What the fuck are you smokin', diarrhea!"

"No, it's your mother's pubes, I got them last night when she was suckin' my dick."

"I hope she swallowed cause my mother drinks cum."

"Word, she swallowed," he says. "And she said you fuckin' taught her how."

Before Tipsy could run Romeo had him in a headlock and Tipsy was saying he's sorry and how he didn't mean it but he's laughing the whole time and Romeo gives him a thousand noogies on the head. Cremont steps out holding a six of 45 and seeing Romeo with his brother in a headlock, Cremont starts poking Tipsy in the stomach and Tipsy begs to be let go and promises he'll never say anything again, but they don't believe him. As people pass Romeo tells them to pop Tipsy in the head, which most of them do, then Romeo squeezes Tipsy's head in his arms and Tipsy yells that his ears are getting crushed but Romeo keeps squeezing and the harder Tipsy fights to break free the tighter Romeo squeezes. It gets serious cause Tipsy's crying and his brother just stands there watching and drinking his beer. Romeo takes an empty can and crushes it against Tipsy's head and Tipsy's real upset and trying with all his might to break free but Romeo just laughs and squeezes harder. Romeo finally releases his grip and Tipsy collapses to the sidewalk holding his red, swollen ears. He looks up to see Romeo and Cremont laughing in his face and he curses them out saying how they're homo-faggot queers who suck each other's dicks and take it up the ass. Romeo makes a move and Tipsy runs down the street as his brother chuckles. Romeo steps into the store and grabs a six of beer and walking past the counter he tells Ravi to put it on his tab, one he doesn't have, but as long as Ravi lets them take free beer, his windows seem to go unbroken. They go to the Pot Store around the corner, and walking in beat like there's a music playing in their heads, they pass Clara Lugo with her humongo tits in view. Romeo chucks her a beer and tells her he'll be back later for his blow job but she tells him to fuck off. In the Pot Store Boots is ringing up two packs of Camels and a lid of sense for a teenage flatchest-whore. As she leaves Romeo tells her cigarettes are bad for her tits.

Brazil lights joint after joint after joint till his lungs ache but he can't get high. He shoots a beer and launches a rocket and if he had a brick he'd beat it against his head cause he still can't get high. They go over to Soby's cause Cremont said he wasn't feeling so good and Soby's lying on the couch with a pain in his spleen and a beer in his hand. Brazil rolls up a joint and cracks up a rocket and sprinkles it inside but Cremont tells him it's a fucking waste to mix blast with weed but Brazil tells him to suck his mother's dick. He lights it and they all toke, even Cremont. Soby's mother comes in from the bedroom and seeing them all smoking and drinking, she goes back inside. Romeo says that they should go make a collection, and no one disagrees. Soby gets up, puts on his pants, takes his medication—three pills too many—and Brazil rips the bottle from his hands and gulps the last seven in one shot. Brazil figured if codeine couldn't get him high, he was probably dead.

On the sidewalk near Becky's building there's a crowd of people standing around something on the ground. Romeo and the others pass to see a dead run-over cat lying there with its eyes closed and its teeth clenched tight and an old lady is crying and Romeo tells her, Lady it's only a fucking cat. Brazil is mesmerized staring at the carcass, and when Romeo calls him he doesn't hear. Romeo's sister Joy turns the corner and seeing her brother and his friends she crosses the street. Soby says he wants to fuck her bad and for a second Romeo thinks about letting him, then he tells them if she agrees they can all fuck her but they can't rape her. Soby called out to her but she ignored them. Brazil stumbled around and could barely walk and his eyes were two red slits. He had foam coming out of his mouth, and by the time they reached cardboard town he threw up on his sneakers. Romeo pointed out the spot where he nearly killed that sack-o-shit and looking around he couldn't find the two-by-four. Tipsy runs by and seeing his brother with Romeo and the others in the lot he calls them a bunch of faggot-nazi-homos-from-hell and that their mothers suck maggot infested moose cock and that he took a dump and it became their fathers. Then he started in with shit that was so weird and bizarre nobody could figure out what the fuck he meant. Brazil took out his gun and aimed it at Tipsy but Cremont grabbed his arm and told him to get a fucking grip. Tipsy ran away out of sight and not a second too soon.

Chantaka was leaning on Caesar's limo parked in front of the Chinese restaurant. She saw Romeo and the others coming by so she stubbed out her cigarette and fingered the beads around her neck. Romeo could smell her sweet perfume as he ran his fingers through her rows of tightly braided hair. He told her she was senfuckingsational and how could she be looking so African in her long colored robe with pounds of beads and chains and still be working for Caesar. Cremont asked if Caesar was wearing purple today and when she said yeah they all laughed. Romeo brushed up so close she could feel his cock against her leg. She stroked it through his pants and gave him a smile. Soby and Brazil stood by without a word cause Chantaka had so much class it made them impotent. Romeo asked her out for a date and she giggled and said she was too old for him but Romeo told her he liked older women and besides, she was only 22. She told him to talk to Caesar about it but he said he wanted a date not an appointment and she giggled again and pinched the tip of his cock. Jimbo came out carrying a bag of noodles and seeing them all around Chantaka he told them to keep their fucking hands off the merchandise but Romeo told him to shut his fucking mouth before he gets hit with a stray bullet from who-knows-where. Jimbo called him a fucking punk and as Romeo made a move Jimbo jumped in the car and locked all the doors. Chantaka giggled and told Romeo to behave himself and he did. Caesar came out wearing a purple tie and Cremont laughed but Caesar didn't know why. He told them to quit fucking around with his driver and what the fuck are they trying to do. Romeo told him he should be fucking thankful for having such a fabulous babe around who can give him class cause he's as cheap as a dirty used scumbag. Caesar called him a poor stupid nigger with no chance of reaching fifteen. He ordered Chantaka into the fucking car, and as she did, she looked at Romeo and from the gleam in her eye he couldn't tell if she was in love with him or just wanted to suck his dick.

Brazil puked twice on his way up the stairs and Romeo was getting pissed. He told him to wait outside but Brazil snapped out of it and said fuck you. They could hear the tv from outside the door. Cremont whispered to hurry up cause he was missing Green Acres. Romeo tapped and a voice called out asking who it is.

"It's the fuckin' Avon lady, she's here to suck your dick."

There was a moment of silence, then Romeo called out, "Well?" The lock was undone and the door slowly opened. Harold Ladley stood there with fear-filled eyes in his thin hollow face, trying to smile. He stepped away and invited them in, asked why they didn't use their key. Romeo told him he was testing him and that so far he's doing good. Cremont went to the couch while Soby went through the drawers while Brazil went to the fridge and upon seeing the food inside he puked on the eggs. Harold asked him if he wanted some Pepto but Brazil just pushed him away. Harold asked Soby to please let him keep the silver crucifix his mother gave him but Soby told him if he wanted it so bad he should've hid it cause anything they find is theirs, then he put it in his pocket. Cremont was yelling from the couch for Harold to get a beer but he didn't have any. Brazil was in the bathroom puking his guts into the bowl. Romeo came in and flushed it, then took a rocket from Brazil's shirt and launched it. He passed the pipe to Harold who took it as an honor and awkwardly toked without inhaling. Romeo told him to give it up and for a second Harold didn't know what that meant. He reached behind the radiator and pulled up his bottle of pills, prescription, anti-depressants, cause Harold was fucked up in the head and always wore a wrist band to cover the scars. Romeo patted his back and Harold laughed and felt like one of the boys. Brazil leaned against the tub and said he wanted to get laid but Romeo laughed in his face and told him he couldn't even get it up and when Harold laughed Brazil got pissed and punched him in the balls. Soby pulled him out of the bathroom and rifled through his pockets and finding only forty bucks he pushed him to the floor. Harold started crying and cowering in the corner and Romeo came over and told him he was sorry, that they didn't mean it. Harold wiped his eyes and Romeo told him they'd be real good friends if Harold had more money and that nobody would hurt him and that he'd be cool and they would even get him laid. Romeo helped him to his feet and with a soothing comfort told Harold to give it up. Harold went to the refrigerator, groaning as he opened it. Beneath the rotting tomatoes in the lettuce drawer was two hundred bucks of disability. Romeo looked at Soby and they both had to grin. Harold handed the money to Romeo who put his arm around him and told him he was doing real good. Romeo told him to go sit in the corner and not to move unless he's told to, and as he did, Soby told him to face the wall. Brazil was lying in the tub with the shower pouring down on him, and he looked over at Romeo like it's fucking normal to be in the tub with your clothes on. Brazil says he wants to get laid and that he could fuck any bitch twelve times more than Romeo no matter how fucked up he is. Romeo gave Soby the two hundred bucks and told him to come back with rockets and Stacy, and when Brazil heard Stacy's name he howled like a dog. As Soby left, Cremont yelled for him to bring back some beer, Colt, not that Old English shit. Cremont sat on the couch watching tv and slicing swastikas in the cushion with his knife. Seeing Harold rock on the floor with his face against the wall, Cremont thought of slicing one into his back but didn't feel like getting up. Romeo sat in the kitchen and launched his last rocket while Brazil was grunting in the bathroom and Romeo didn't even want to know what the fuck he was doing in there. Romeo started drifting into his mind and thinking about Becky and wishing she was here. He should've told Soby to bring her back too but she would never come and if she did they'd probably all want to fuck her and he would have to kill them with his shiny gold gun before he'd let that happen and then he remembered that there was something he had to do for Sammy and that was probably the only reason Sammy gave him the gun to begin with. He thought of killing his mother and ditching her body cause it was all her fault for getting herself stuck in a situation where all she had to give them was nothing. It was her fault for Ledell and Rodney too, and everytime she and his sister look at him with their accusing eyes he wants to dump acid in their fucking faces and see how they like it. He wonders how he could be so fucked up cause he can't remember being any other way. What is it inside that drives him crazy and makes him do these things, makes him enjoy it. No matter what they think, he tried to look out for his brothers, taught them what he could. And he missed them, especially Ledell. Fucking Ledell. He didn't do nothing to nobody and didn't deserve it and if it were possible Romeo would've taken that bullet instead. And shit, he's gotta find the fucking motherfucker cause everyday that passes makes it a little harder to do. But he can't ask Sammy for help till that other little matter is cleared up first. Romeo felt himself coming down as the tingle left his legs and the floor grew from his feet, and seeing Harold rocking like a retard in the corner, he wanted to hurt him somehow, maybe kill him.

Soby floats in with Stacy behind and he puts the bag on the couch and takes out twenty three rockets and Stacy almost cums in her pants when she sees them. Romeo took a look at Stacy and with her new short-crop wannabe-a-man look, he thought she made a big mistake. She still had a great ass. Brazil steps out of the bathroom and Stacy asks if he likes her new haircut and he tells her she looks like a fucking ubangi-man from the jungle and before she can respond she's drawn to the lit match. The scene became an orgy of drugs and wild sex cause Stacy was fucking and sucking everybody from everywhere and they were doing geometric combinations and going four at once and setting Olympic records and Stacy was fucked out of her face and as long as they were firing, she was fucking. Harold stayed in the corner the whole time and Soby told him if he even glanced back they would cut off his dick and stick it up his ass, so Harold just sat there and cried against the wall. Brazil pissed out of the window and Cremont says what the fuck are you doing there might be kids down there and Brazil tells him to come over and drink it if he don't like it. Romeo sits up cause he can't take anymore and his body's aching and screaming for a break and he doesn't know how the fuck Stacy's doing it cause she's taking on twice as much. Soby turns her over and fucks her doggie style and as he's doing it he's banging her head against the wall. Hearing her head against the wall and her deep breathing and the helpless tremor in her voice, Romeo's cock gets hard and his head spins and he feels a power inside that makes him want to destroy the universe. He puts on his pants and goes over to Harold, lifting him by the hair to his feet. Harold starts bawling real loud and Romeo smacks him hard across the face. Soby sees that look in Romeo's eye and pulls out of Stacy who collapses in a ball and asks what's wrong. Romeo bounces Harold off the wall and punches him in the throat and Harold's choking and heaving up his tongue and Romeo stands over him and tells him to act like a man. Harold tries to crawl away but Romeo grabs the back of his shirt and lifts him to the couch, rolls him over, rips his shirt off and throws it across the room. Harold starts flipping out and screaming with his face in the ripped cushions of the couch and Romeo starts kicking him in the side over and over and over and when Brazil steps out of the bedroom he's smiling like a fucking clown. Harold is buried in the couch and Brazil takes over when Romeo is out of breath. Romeo looks through the kitchenette for something else to use as Brazil tries to pull Harold's face out of the cushion but it won't come. Brazil grabs a handful of hair and rips the head back and before Harold can bury it again,

Brazil clocks him one in the cheek. Romeo tosses him a pair of scissors and he starts clumsily chopping at Harold's hair, violently pulling it and cutting and Brazil doesn't care if he's cutting scalp and ear in between. He starts slicing lines in the soft of his back and Harold whirls around screaming with his face all bent and contorted and he doesn't look human anymore. Brazil grabs Cremont's sneaker from the floor and shoves it with all his might into Harold's mouth and holds it there till Harold's eyes are bugging and his arms twitching and his face burning and just as he's about to black out, Brazil pulls it free. Harold's gasping and choking for air and Romeo comes over and tells him if he tries to scream again they'll kill him. Stacy comes out of the bedroom with Cremont and Soby, a cloud of smoke following. Harold quivered like a nude in Alaska and Soby told Stacy he'd fire another if she blows Harold and Stacy looks over at pathetic little Harold who's not even aware of them standing there. She tells Soby to take his pants off and he and Cremont both take a leg and pull till Harold's in his dirty stretched-out jockeys. Soby tells Stacy she'll have to do the rest and she kneels in front and pulls down his shorts and Harold's staring straight ahead like a zombie as she takes him in her mouth. Harold gets hit in the chest with an egg and when everybody looks over Romeo stands at the sink rinsing off the eggs and chucking them at Harold. Brazil grabs a couple and smashes them on Harold's head. Stacy quits sucking cause by now Soby's firing and after taking her toke, she goes to the fridge and starts taking out things to throw at Harold and soon everybody's into the act and they're grabbing everything in sight and chucking it at Harold who sits there bare and gets covered with eggs and ketchup and mustard and cheese and lettuce and baloney and french dressing and jelly and ice cubes and when the fridge is empty they start chucking from the cabinets and now Harold was wearing rice and spaghetti and cereal and oatmeal and pancake mix and all kinds of spices and shit, Romeo couldn't believe how much food there was. When there was no more they went for the forks and knives and the first four just bounced off his head but the fifth one caught him in the shoulder and stuck there and Harold wailed but this time not so loud. Brazil grabbed some forks and tried to imbed them then Stacy grabbed some and soon it became a dart game with all of them tossing forks and chipping out pieces of Harold's flesh. Romeo felt a rush inside, beyond drugs and sex and his cock was hard and throbbing and he was about to cum any second so he grabbed Stacy and made her suck him as he continued chucking forks and as he's chucking he realizes this is as close to heaven as you can get. Just as he shot his load he popped Harold in the side of the head. Stacy had cum pouring out of her mouth and Harold had blood pouring out of his ear. Brazil got tired of throwing things so he grabbed the empty drawer and smashed it over Harold's head; cutting himself on the splinters. Brazil kicked him in the face and Harold cuddled up in a tight little ball whimpering and making sounds they'd never heard before. Soby and Cremont stood to the side frying their brains and enjoying the show. Romeo sat on the windowsill and tried to catch his breath, then stood up and pissed in the oven. Harold stopped moving and just lay there still for a minute and Cremont got real nervous. Soby went over and hearing him breathe told Cremont to relax, that Harold was just in a coma. They all laughed, including Stacy, and Brazil searched under the sink for something. He came up with a can of Drano and turning around he told them he had the perfect cure for coma-ism. While Romeo, Soby, and Cremont thought he was gonna dump it in Harold's mouth, Brazil was more creative than that. They watched him fill a pot with water and dump it on Harold's body, then he sprinkled Drano crystals all over and Soby told him what the fuck is that supposed to do but Brazil just gave him a slimy smile and told him to be patient, motherfucker. And sure enough, after a minute, Soby noticed a dark fog hovering over Harold's body and worse than that was the sizzling sound coming from it. There was a twitch and a spasm and in a fucking eruption of blisters Harold's skin was ripping in seams and he wakes with a scream that makes even Stacy feel something inside, but the others are laughing and joking and pointing like they're watching channel 13. Harold jumps to his feet and stumbles to the bathroom but Brazil trips him up and he lands in a heap on the floor, Romeo thought he heard an arm snap. Harold crumbles in the tub and the water shoots out and the whole time he's screaming like it's the end of the world and Cremont tells them they'd better shut him up cause somebody might call the cops. Brazil pulls his gun out but Romeo grabs his arm and tells him why kill something that has free drugs and money. Brazil puts his gun away, but Romeo takes out his and everybody's wondering what the fuck's going on and as Romeo goes over to the bathroom they follow cause if he's gonna kill Harold they want to see it. Romeo shows Harold the gun and tells him if he doesn't shut up right this second he'll shoot him in the eyes. Harold stops screaming and starts sobbing in a towel and all across his back and sides you could see bleeding red craters and Soby tells them the shit is still burning in. He launched a rocket and they all just stood there watching and toking, and once Harold started weakly moaning with every wheezing breath cause he was too tired to sob, they decided to go. Turning out of the bathroom Soby asks Brazil ain't you gonna piss on him and Brazil says why should he and Soby says ain't that your style. Brazil tells him to suck his father's pussy and they all laugh. In the hall Romeo wondered how much longer he could live like this, cause it felt like he'd already lived a lifetime and it was only five in the afternoon.

Joy was cooking chicken in the kitchen. She didn't look away from the stove as he came in. Romeo went to his room and put his gun away. The smell of roasting chicken seeped through the walls and under the floorboards. He was starving, so he went inside and told Joy he was staying to eat but she didn't say a word. Looking at her tight hateful face he wanted to tell her who the fuck does she think she is and it's his money that pays for the food and the rent and no matter how much they hate him, they still take his money. Instead he sat at the crooked wooden table with his initials carved in the top, and at the next place, he fingered the sloppy L weakly cut into the wood till Joy put a dish down over it. Romeo asked her if she sucked anybody's cock today and how did it taste. She called him a fucking low-life degenerate and how could he do that shit to Debbie Carter but Romeo told her they didn't do anything she didn't want done. Joy said go

fuck yourself; he called her a fucking cheap-lesbo
whore with a pussy the size of New Jersey. She
tried to smash a plate over his head but he blocked it
with his arm and she started screaming about how
he murdered Ledell and that he might as well have
pulled the trigger himself cause it was all his fault
and they warned him but he wouldn't fucking listen
cause he's a cold blooded brother-killer and everyfuckingthing he touches gets destroyed. Romeo
goes nuts and pops her in the face and they go at it
with fists and feet and Joy kicks him in the balls but
he punches her with all his might in the tits and she
falls to the floor crying and choking and clutching
her tit and when their mother steps in and starts
calling Romeo an animal and a monster and yelling
how could he beat his sister like that and does it
make him feel like a man, Romeo didn't want to tell
her that it did. Joy got up threatening death and
cancer and ran out of the apartment. Romeo ripped
a leg from the bird and ate it on his way outside.

Pepperton was supposed to be coming out of
the pool hall sometime tonight, and while Romeo
watched from across the street, Brazil stood on
the corner, just in case. Romeo had his gold-plated
gun and it was primed and ready and so was he
cause the bullets were talking to him and telling
him to make sure he doesn't miss. The trigger told
him to take off the safety, and he did. Romeo took a

deep breath and started psyching up, picturing scenes of Pepperton doing fucked up things to people he liked, people like Becky, and Rodney, and Ledell, then back to Becky, and after a minute Pepperton started changing into this monster that Romeo found very easy to hate. Pepperton comes out but he's with some guy wearing a beret. Romeo looks to Brazil. Pepperton talks with this guy on the steps and he's moving and talking with his hands and from across the street Romeo couldn't hear what they were saying. Brazil looked back and Romeo could tell he was thinking they should take them both out. After a few minutes, Amboy Sanford comes by and starts talking to the guy with the beret. They both go inside leaving Pepperton by himself. Pepperton stepped away and started down the street, Romeo was tingling all over, higher than any rocket could ever take him. This was it. This was a hit. And hits were special. With his soft rubber Jordans on the pavement he followed Pepperton as Brazil watched from the corner. Out of nowhere the guy with the beret comes back down the stairs and stands there watching Pepperton being followed by Romeo. Brazil leans against the wall and once he sees the guy following Romeo, Brazil steps out and follows him. Now there's a fucking parade of killers following each other and it looks like the Marx Brothers from hell. Romeo sneaks closer and Brazil does too and Pepperton and his friend haven't heard a thing yet. Suddenly from behind there's a click and a shot and Pepperton whirls around with his gun and starts firing but Romeo jumps down to the pavement firing back and he hits Pepperton twice in the chest and once in the face and even in the dark he could see the white of Pepperton's skull coming through his shattered cheeks. Behind him Brazil pumped two more shots into the other guy who was lying on the ground. Then Brazil pulled off the guy's beret and shot him point blank in the head. Romeo thought of putting one in Pepperton's head but by now people were screaming and calling for help. They took off down the street and cut through the back yards. Climbing the brick wall behind the OTB Romeo turned around and was alone. Brazil was on the other side trying to climb up and Romeo told him to hurry. Brazil was grunting and struggling and just as his arm reached the top Romeo grabbed it and helped him over. Romeo sees a growing red patch on Brazil's side and Brazil is trying to act like nothing's wrong. Romeo tells him he's been shot and Brazil makes like he didn't even know it. They move through the streets keeping out of sight and by the time they reach the houses they can hear sirens slicing through the night. Romeo helps Brazil into the elevator and they ride up to the tenth floor where Soby's waiting in his apartment. Soby lets them in then says shit what the fuck happened and Brazil says he cut himself shaving. They sit him on the faded dirty couch and they rip off his shirt and there's a tiny dime-size hole with a second degree burn around it, and it's dripping like a leaky faucet. Soby gets a towel from the kitchen and puts it against the cushion of the couch, then his mother steps out and seeing Brazil with no shirt and a bullet hole in his side, turns and goes back inside without a word. Romeo asks Brazil how the fuck he got shot and Brazil tells him about the guy following and that just as the guy raised his gun, Brazil popped him in the back and that's when Pepperton started shooting and though Pepperton may have missed Romeo, he sure as hell didn't miss Brazil. Soby said maybe they should take him to the hospital but Romeo said no way cause how are they gonna explain a bullet in the side. Romeo went out and found Becky cause she knew about first aid from when she was a girl scout. She looked at the wound and said Brazil should go to the hospital cause it could get infected but Romeo told her to do what she could. She cleaned it and dabbed it and covered it with gauze. Romeo launched a rocket which they all toked. Brazil fell asleep on the floor and while Romeo and Soby got fucked out of their faces, Becky cleaned the blood off the couch with vinegar and water.

That afternoon Romeo could feel all eyes on him as he passed, from the upper windows and the open storefronts and all the whores and the zooka boys and everybody must've known cause he felt a thousand burning lasers melting into him, but no one said a word. Soby and Cremont showed him the article in the paper saying how it was just another example of the violent and deadly world of drugs, and seeing as how Pepperton probably had it coming anyway, Romeo knew it would be quickly forgotten. Except by Sammy. Cause Sammy would remember. The next thing to do now is find who did Ledell and take care of that. Sammy would help. As Romeo walked past the school and saw the empty yard, he thought of firing into the windows and playing death roulette. Maybe he would hit Becky and what are the fucking odds of that happening and if it did, then it was meant to be. Brazil was staying at Stacy's place and he sat there with his gun out in case Stacy's husband decided to show up. His side was all fucked up and the bullet was still inside and no matter how bad it hurt, Brazil pretended it didn't. When Stacy asked if she could fuck him he said he was too tired but she could blow him instead, which she did, and everytime she took him in deep a drop of blood would pump out of his side till the bandage was soaking wet with red. Romeo and the others stopped by and launched their brains into space and Brazil got up and tried to dance. He bumped into the couch and his gun fell to the floor and fired just missing Cremont's leg but hitting a cabinet in the kitchen. Romeo grabbed the gun and took out the bullets and told Brazil to fucking sit down before he kills one of them. They all laughed as the hallway filled with questions. When the news came on at 11, they all sat around the fuzzy black and white with a coat hanger for an antenna, listening to the Lady in Blue with her mike in front of the pool hall reporting the vicious drug deaths and how one guy was mutilated with bullets and that now there's probably gonna be a major drug war. They all looked at Brazil and laughed cause it was no drug war Lady, it was just the way Brazil is. She reports how Pepperton had been identified as a Colombian trying to set himself up in the neighborhood, and all at once a light clicked inside Romeo's head and things became very clear. The whole story about bad shit and Pepperton wanting his money back was bullshit cause Sammy wanted him out for trying to move in. Though Romeo felt betrayed in a way, there was nothing he could do about it, so he launched another rocket. While the others watched tv and Brazil slept on the couch, he took Stacy inside and they fucked and sucked till they both passed out.

Brazil's side was completely red by the morning, it was almost glowing, and when Stacy put a cool rag to it he almost passed out. Romeo said they still couldn't take him to a hospital, not so soon after the hit. Brazil called Cremont a fucking pussy for even suggesting it, and Romeo said Brazil was right, Cremont is a fucking pussy but Cremont said fuck you and took out some rockets and launched them as Stacy sat on his lap. Brazil got up holding his side and went to the bathroom. Soby turned on the tv but couldn't get a picture and Romeo told them all to shut up as the news came on. They briefly mention the vicious drug hit then move on to the weather, and Romeo knew it would be old news by tomorrow.

Soby came by with Ralphie from the pharmacy with his doctor's bag to check Brazil's wound. He sticks his eye up close and tries to look inside but all he sees is red meat and blood and as he touches it with his finger Brazil grimaces with a smile. Ralphie pulls out all kinds of shit from his bag and playing doctor he checks pressures and heartbeats and Romeo knows he doesn't know what the fuck he's doing but he looks professional doing it. They pass him the pipe and after a toke he says the wound is bad but not too bad cause he doesn't think anything is really damaged, it's just that the bullet is wedged in there somehow. He tells Stacy to keep it clean and keep him high and before leaving he asks if anyone wants a shot of morphine. Romeo gives him a lid of sense but Ralphie turns it down. Brazil calls him Doctor Dickhead as he goes out the door.

That night Romeo went to Luckyfoot's but the zooka boys said he wasn't in and when Romeo asked when's he coming back they didn't know. Kenny Carter says what the fuck d'you do to my sister and Romeo turned with a glare and told him to shut his fucking mouth before they do the same to him. As Kenny went to say something else Romeo popped him in the face and two of the zooka boys took a step till Romeo turned to face them, and though he was outnumbered five to one, none of them made a move. On his way back to Stacy's Romeo wondered what was up cause something wasn't right about this: Luckyfoot never went out. And the zooka boys never dissed him like that. He got this eerie feeling that he was being watched, and as he clung close to the buildings he looked for any sign of being followed. Caesar's limo drove past and looking in the dark tinted windows he couldn't see if Chantaka was with him or not.

Stacy's door was ajar but hearing the tv inside Romeo thought they were just being careless. Once inside he found the place empty and the cushions from the couch were on the floor and a table was moved and Romeo ran to the kitchen and got his gun from the drawer, then locked the door. With his brain on survive he crept into the bedroom but that was empty too. So was the bathroom. Romeo ran scenes in his head of what could've happened and how there must've been a good explanation but his instincts told him differently. All this shit is happening cause of Sammy and if Sammy doesn't do something to stop it right here and now, Romeo's gonna take him out with his gold-handled gun. Wouldn't that be justice. He hears a noise in the hall and he backs against the wall and the first face through that door is gonna be choking on bullets. A key is fit into the lock but it won't turn, and Romeo hears a foreign cursing voice that he doesn't recognize so he cocks the gun. The doorjamb snaps and the door swings open and a huge guy in a turban steps in and seeing Romeo he reaches for his belt but Romeo shoots him in the stomach. As he crumples to the floor Romeo rips the gun from his hand and points it in his face. The guy is cursing and groaning and Romeo hysterically asks where Brazil and the others are but the guy doesn't know what the fuck he's talking about. The guy asks for his wife and Romeo tells him she ain't here. Everybody in the hall starts yelling and threatening to call the cops and Romeo hops over the body and tells him he's sorry it was all a big mistake and the guy just lies there holding his guts and moaning for Stacy.

Romeo took off through the back lots and yards and this was a new feeling for him cause he always played the hunter not the hunted. Cutting through cardboard town two bums ran screaming for their lives at the sight of him. All he could think of was finding somebody who could tell him something, somebody he could trust but there was nobody, not if Brazil and the others were gone. The only person he could think of was Becky but she wouldn't know anything and he wouldn't want her involved even if she did. He ran to the houses and snuck up to Soby's using the stairs and standing outside the door he kept his gun tucked under his arm ready to shoot. Soby's mother saw the gun but said nothing, she just told him Soby wasn't home. He brushed past her and grabbed the phone without asking. She closed the door and went into the kitchen as he dialed and after several rings Joy answered and he tried to be cool.

"Yo Joy, what's up?"

"What did you do," she spits out with urgency.

"What do you mean?"

"There were some guys here looking for you, then the cops. What did you do!"

"Nothin', I didn't do nothin'. Who was there?"

Then after a pause, "Where are you," she asked, and Romeo felt this chill inside cause they might've been there with her. He didn't answer.

"Look, you fucked up bad this time," she says. "Whatever you did, don't bring it here, you hear me. Don't come home, cause momma's upset as it is. You hear?"

"Don't fuckin' tell me what to do!"

"Why don't you go fuck yourself?!"

"No fuck you! You cunt! I'm sendin' some guys over to fuckin' beat your..." At that Joy hung up. When Romeo put the phone down his hand was shaking and from the kitchen he could see Soby's mother watching from the crack in the door. He didn't know what to do, where to go. He grabbed the phone again and called Becky but she wasn't home. He hung up and left the apartment.

The key turned in the lock and this time the door wasn't chained. Peeking in he was hit with a stench that burned out his nose but he quickly scurried in and locked the door behind. The place was the way they left it and taking another step in Romeo knew why. Rutherford was lying in his bed stiff and dead, his skin blue, his eyes shut but his mouth was open like he died in the middle of a snore. Romeo stood right over him looking for a wound or bullet hole but there was nothing. So Rutherford went out peaceful, he thought. He wrapped him in the shit-stained sheets and left him on the bed till he could figure out what to do. He went to turn on the tv but remembered they chucked it out the window. There was no radio, no phone, nothing, and Romeo had no way of knowing what was going on, so he sat in the bedroom overlooking the street and watched out the window for any sign of trouble. At ten after four he snuck out of the apartment and went to the pay-phone and called Becky, told her old man to wake her. After a minute her groggy voice says where the fuck are you. Romeo tells her he's in trouble but she already knows cause the cops are out looking for him and when he asks why she tells him something about that guy from the brick houses named Harry and all of a sudden he thinks of Harold. A cop car turns the corner two blocks up and he tells her where he's staying and to come over but don't be followed. He hangs up and creeps into the building. An hour later Becky taps and he cautiously lets her in and asks her what happened and she tells him that Harold was found by somebody from Social Services who came by to check on him and when they called the cops and an ambulance took him away he died but not before mentioning names. Romeo tells her he didn't do it and they were only fooling around and that Harold was perfectly fine when they left him. She believes him. He tells her about Brazil and the others and she gets tense and tells him there have been some strange people hanging around. She asks him what's that smell and he opens the door and shows her Rutherford and when she almost pukes at the sight, he smiles and tells her it was from natural causes. She asks him what to do and he says they'll steal a car and get away, the two of them, just get out of the whole fucking state. Drive to Georgia. They'll be safe there. Becky tells him he's crazy and that they can't just drive from state to state and maybe if he explains to the cops what really happened they'll understand. Romeo tells her he can't do that, but he doesn't explain why. He tells Becky they'll need some things and he scribbles out a list and he gives her two hundred bucks in twenties and tells her to blow half on rockets.

He found some ammonia under the sink and dumped it on Rutherford's body cause the smell was getting worse. He sat by the window and stayed out of view as he watched all the cops and the creeps driving through. Maybe he could chuck Rutherford's body down in the alley, it would only have to be there till tonight cause by then they'll be gone. Romeo saw two of the younger zooka boys walking past and he wanted to shoot them from the window. He checked out parked cars cause he would have to take one from this block and maybe he could even take one of Sammy's or Luckyfoot's and wouldn't that be a good sendoff. He tuned in the radio that Becky brought from home and after three different news reports he started thinking that maybe all this shit was taking place in his head. There was no mention of anything about Pepperton or drug wars or Harold or Stacy's husband—nothing. It was as if none of it ever happened. Maybe this was all one big fucked up nightmare and Romeo would wake up tomorrow in his bed and everything would be normal and he'd fight with Joy and watch his mother cry then go out with his friends and get high. Becky tapped twice then kicked with her foot, and Romeo let her in. She was all out of breath and saying how Parker told her that Stacy had been found in the trunk of a car and how at first nobody could identify her cause she wasn't pregnant but the girl in the trunk was. When they cut her open they found Brazil's head stuffed inside. Now Romeo knew for sure what he was dealing with, cause Pepperton was more than just a mild annoyance, Pepperton had some big friends back home. Becky was shaking in her skin and Romeo grabbed her shoulders and told her everything was cool and that it has nothing to do with her and that as soon as the sun goes down they're gone. He launched two rockets in a row and sat back listening to Funky DJ Rap-Dog scream about a white racist world and how niggers don't stand a chance. Becky glanced over with a blitzed-out smile and they both had to laugh at the crazy shit he gets himself into. She got up and came behind his chair and started rubbing his back and squeezing his shoulders and rubbing his cock and telling him he's too tense and for a second he wondered what the fuck he was getting her mixed up in, and why. She made some sandwiches of ham and baloney and they ate them in the waning light of day. Becky told him she had to stop home and get some things and when Romeo tried to stop her she turned and told him she loved him and would do anything and go anywhere with him but first she was saying goodbye to her mother. He knew there was no stopping her so he let her go. The news came on and told of a woman found dead in the trunk of a car but they didn't mention her by name; they called it a homicide.

Becky never came back. After two hours of pacing and launching and gripping his gun and running to the window at every sound in the street, there was still no sign of her. Maybe she changed her mind or maybe they paid her off or maybe they caught her and were cutting her up and stuffing things up her pussy. Of the three possibilities he hoped it was the third cause Becky would never betray him would she? He watches Rutherford decay on the soaking sheets and if anything else oozes out of his fucking body he's getting tossed in the alley.

Sammy played this one perfectly, like a fucking violinist. He got everything he wanted. Romeo couldn't even go to the cops cause he'd have to face the Harold rap and there was no way he could do time with Sammy's friends in prison. This must be terror, he thought. He'd never felt it before. Not like this anyway. Not where everything inside of you is screaming to live but you know that's kind of impossible now. He sat there in the dark trying to picture death and what it would be like and if there really is a god. He told god to go fuck himself, cause he's not ashamed of anything he ever did cause next to this whole fucking empty black world of misery poverty hopelessness and loss where even burning in hell has to be a step up, it was minor. And fuck anybody that don't like it cause they can fuck their mothers and their homo-fathers and rip their cocks off and eat their guts and flush themselves down the fucking sewer and rot with the shit cause he's going out in style. And Sammy and Pepperton can fuck each other up the ass for all he cares. He sat facing the door and holding his gun and frying his brain on his last rocket and the room seemed to get smaller as the walls moved in closer and the ceiling got lower and everything darker and the first motherfucker through that door gets his dick shot off. Then Romeo closed his eyes and waited for destiny.

CELLBLOCK SERENADE

"**Fuck you.** And Fuck your mother too. Then punch her pussy when she's havin' her period and drink the poison blood. And choke on it and let it drip down your fuckin' lungs and seep into your icy black heart till you drown on your own cancerous bile. Cause you don't know shit. You sit in your fuckin' high handed perches like judges and juries when none of you have ever lived a day in your fuckin' lives. Not a real day. Not my kind of day. You go out to your restaurants and drink bottled water and watch tv in your nice comfy homes in your chic fashioned clothes with your bottle of wine and your things and belongings all standin' by ready and waitin' to click on the fuckin' remote till you blitz out on sitcoms and fall off to hell. And may the next stray bullet have your name on it. Fuck you.

And Fuck your mother too. Fuck Fuck Fuck shit-tin' cocksucker bastard cunt and fuckin' shit cock cunt tits pussy pussy pussy cuntfuck, you mother-fuckin' uterus bitch whore cunt, cunt, twat-fuck pussy-cunt. Fuck Fuck Fuck and die motherfucker die motherfucker die motherfucker die.''

CONFUSION ON BLASTOFF STREET

Pedro said he saw Londa's ghost floating down the street but nobody believed him cause he was on acid at the time and suddenly his insides poured out of his mouth in a flood of intestines and Miss Lonely just swam up from the goo and said hello and looking around at the street and the people on it she said she'd rather be dead and dove back down but her open-toe shoe was left floating along in the gutter till Manny kicked it on his way home from prison and it bounced along the curb till a dog ran up and took it away just as Georgie hobbled by with this moonie kind of look on his face cause he still hasn't landed and as shit keeps happening Nancy keeps copping and it's been a lot longer than just the holidays and there seems to be no let-up in sight and her husband still doesn't know shit and he must be out of his fucking mind or else he has a mistress and speaking of mistresses Marybeth is working for a fantasy firm where she doesn't have to do anything but be different people and sometimes dress up as a nazi but it's cool cause they're into it and she's not shooting anymore just doing rockets and Susie's been in a coma for two months at the children's ward off Seventh cause when Chas found out that Willy ran away he really flipped out and beat the shit out of mommy and Susie and he punched Susie once too hard in the face and Willy doesn't know anything about this cause he's still on his way to someplace that doesn't exist and lately he's been finding out that sometimes you have to be a girl if you wanna eat and Chuckie thought he saw a porcupine on his foot till it disappeared and became his spleen and picking it up he strolls through the danger like that Colt 45 guy from those beer commercials till somebody said there were these guys from hell doing things to people that were too fucked up to imagine and they were deadly motherfuckers with the hearts of cockroaches and faces to match and the story of Drano-Face Harold still makes people shake their heads and it's amazing how Fat Tony the Wop is taking credit for their disappearance and he swears he was in on it and it was done by a friend of his named Alfie from Newark and Whitey the Cop drove by and

Tony shut his mouth and Whitey's wondering what the fuck a white guy's doing living here cause he must be out of his fucking mind then Whitey turned to his new partner Officer Washington and laughed to himself cause it was bound to happen eventually and maybe it was his punishment for being so fucked up and Richard the Executive is getting divorced cause his wife found those pictures of him dressed as a whore with Tito Mendez shoving his dick in his mouth and all the lying and denying can't erase those pictures and as the chemists got cheaper Sammy got richer like a wave of diarrhea sweeping through the city and everybody's smoking his shit and frying their brains and killing their mothers and raping their sisters and robbing and stealing and stabbing and bleeding and shitting and pissing and slicing their fucking wrists cause no matter how much they smoke it's not enough and as flaming kids run through the streets with baseball wounds and blast-head burns the bullets wizz and splat their guts and mothers cry in infant arms their babies hooked and shooting charms but quitting seems so far away and who-the-fuck wants to anyway with no escape and no reprieve and fuck this world I wanna leave and everything that we've been told is fucking lies and money's gold and god is dead he never lived he left us here and fucked us good and I can't take it anymore I can't take it anymore I can't take it anymore and God please exist and take me the fuck away from here somehow just rip me from this fucking world and take me someplace where it won't hurt so much cause the visions and nightmares and visions and nightmares and nightmares and nightmares and...Fuck me I wanna die.

A B O U T T H E A U T H O R

Buddy Giovinazzo lives in New York
City. He has been making films for
twelve years and currently teaches
filmmaking at the College of Staten
Island. He also likes to play with
sharp objects.